mended hearts

PERFECTLY IMPERFECT

GREER RYLIE

also by greer rylie

- Petals & Steel
- Before Autumn Ends
- Her Accidental Fiancé
- Something More

Mended Hearts

Copyright © 2024 by Greer Rylie

All rights reserved.

<u>**DISCLAIMER**</u>

This book is not meant to be used, nor should it be used, to diagnose or treat any medical or psychological condition. Readers are advised to consult their own medical advisors whose responsibility it is to determine the condition of, and best treatment for, the reader.

Maxine stared down at the dotted line on the document in front of her. Her heart pounded in sync with the ticking clock on Kayla's desk, and she swallowed against the dryness in her throat.

Leaning in, Kayla tapped the contract with one long perfectly manicured fingernail. "If I can just get your signature here, here, and... right here, we can complete the transfer of the deed, and you can officially take possession of the property."

Maxine nodded slowly as she held the pen poised over the first line next to her typed-out name. Her heart thrummed harder beneath her ribs in a mixture of fear, anticipation, joy, and apprehension. Looking up, she met the eyes of the woman sitting across from her. "This isn't a stupid idea, right?" When the other woman remained quiet, Maxine's eyes widened, and she felt a sudden sense of doubt fill her mind. "Kayla, tell me I'm not making a mistake."

Folding her hands on the desk in front of her, Kayla tilted her head to the side and stared at the young woman sitting across from her. "As your friend, I hate the thought of you moving clear across the country and trust me I would keep you here if I could, but I'm not the right person to be asking. As your realtor, I won't try to talk you out of it. You're my best friend, Max, but this sort of commission isn't something I can just let slip through my fingers because of my own selfish wants. The real question is, do *you* think you're making a mistake?"

Maxine's eyes drifted up to the image of the cabin she was about to sign off on. She smiled, feeling the doubt melt away and a calmness filled her. The thought of escaping her hectic city life brought a serene joy she hadn't felt in years. Shaking her head, she turned her attention back to the papers in front of her. "No. I think this is the best thing I've done in a long time."

Kayla remained silent and watched as Maxine signed the contract that would transfer ownership of the cabin and the land it sat on. When Maxine pushed the papers in her direction, she picked them up and flipped through them once more before tapping them on the desk and smiling across at her friend. "Congratulations, Miss Prescott. You just bought yourself a mountain."

Flattening her hand over her stomach, Maxine tried to smile back. "I think I might throw up."

Laughing, Kayla pulled open her bottom desk drawer and laid the contract inside before removing the envelope that contained the keys and other documents the previous owner had sent her. Getting to her feet, she held the envelope out to Maxine as she spoke. "No time to be sick. We have to go out and celebrate you being a new landowner."

The smile slowly faded from Maxine's face as she took the envelope, and she bit down on her bottom lip to keep herself from blurting out the real reason she had decided to move away from the city. Taking a deep breath through her nose, she smiled at Kayla and shook her head as she stood. "I'll have to take a rain check, Kayla. I need to find some boxes so I can start packing, not to mention scheduling shut-off dates for the utilities, and all the things one does before moving."

"Are you sure? We can get lunch and then go get some..." Her words trailed off when Maxine shook her head again.

"Thank you, but I really can't." She followed Kayla with her eyes as she began straightening up the file folders on her desk. Guilt gnawed at her and she sighed before speaking again. "As much as I'd love to join you, I seriously need to start preparing to move. If all goes as planned, I'll be packed, loaded, and on the road by next weekend."

Kayla's eyes widened and her hands stilled. "You're not going to drive a moving van yourself, are you?"

Maxine snorted and chuckled. "Nooooo. I've got a moving company lined up. They're just waiting for confirmation and a start date. Speaking of which..." Pulling her phone from her pocket, she scrolled to the moving company's name and, after seeing Kayla dip her head in a slight nod, tapped it before placing the phone to her ear. When her call was answered she spoke in a cheerful voice. "Good afternoon. This is Maxine Prescott. I called a few days ago about hiring your company. Yes. Right, that's me. Do you have a team available that can start next Saturday morning?" She gave Kayla a thumbs up as she listened to the person on the other end of the call. "8 a.m. will be perfect. Thank you." Lowering the phone, she ended the call and gave Kayla a small smile. "Thank you for handling this for me and for finding the property."

Hurrying around her desk, Kayla held her hand

out and, after shaking Maxine's hand, pulled her in for a hug. "I'm going to miss you so damn much."

Returning her friend's hug, Maxine swallowed down her own churning emotions before stepping back. "If you want, you can stop by the house this week and we'll have that drink. I'll give you a walk through and you can take any notes you need in order to sell the place."

Gasping, Kayla laid a hand over her chest. "You're asking me to sell your house?"

"Absolutely. Of course, at a higher commission rate than your usual fee. If there's a buyer's fee, I'm willing to pay that as well out of what the house sells for." Turning towards the door, she spoke over her shoulder as she continued. "We can discuss the specifics over those drinks." Stepping from the office, she turned once more to smile at Kayla as she pulled the door closed and released a deep breath before looking down at the envelope she held. Her hands shook as she opened it and reached inside for the keys. Pulling them out, she stared down at them before curling her fingers around them tightly. Closing her eyes, she drew in a shuddering breath and released it slowly. Her heart raced again, this time with excitement, and she pressed her fisted hand against her chest as an all too familiar pain flared to life beneath her ribs.

Writing the word 'Dishes' on the box she had just taped shut, Maxine capped the black marker and looked around the kitchen at the empty cupboards. "Looks like that's it in here."

"Are you sure you don't want to keep any of this?"

Maxine turned her head slightly and smiled at Kayla when she looked up. "I'm positive. If there's anything in those boxes that you want or that you think someone can use, you're more than welcome to take it. Otherwise, it'll be taken out by the clean-up crew later."

Kayla chewed the inside of her cheek as she bent over one of the boxes that had the word **'give away'** scrawled across the side. "I have a friend that's starting over, and she could use all the extra household items she can get." Digging through the box closest to her, she pulled out a brand-new vanilla-scented candle and sniffed it before looking back at Maxine. "You're certain you want to get rid of all of this?"

Laughing softly, Maxine waved her hand towards the box. "I don't want any of it. If you think your friend could use all of it, I'll help you load it into your car."

Chuckling, Kayla shook her head. "I'll take all of it, but there's no way it'll all fit in my car." Replacing the candle, she closed the top of the box before brushing her hands together. "Tell you what I'll do. I'll run home and bring the truck back to get all of this. Then, I'll help you finish the packing upstairs."

"Okay, but fair warning, you may be making multiple trips because I'm sure there will be a lot more that I'll be getting rid of before we are done."

Kayla paused and crossed one arm over her chest, using it as a prop for her other arm as she rubbed her chin. "Maybe I'll take some of this over now and see if she wants to come back with me. That is if it's all right with you."

"The more the merrier." Lifting a box, she watched Kayla pick up the one she had been looking through and followed her friend towards the front of the house. As they walked through the living room, Maxine felt a lump forming in her throat. As excited as she was about moving, she knew she would miss the house that had been her home for the last eight years.

The next day, Maxine and Kayla spent the entire morning sorting through the remaining items in the house, deciding what to keep, what to give away, and what to throw out. The memories attached to each item made the task both easier and more difficult. There were moments of laughter as they reminisced about past events, and moments of silence when they came across something particularly sentimental.

After a short break for lunch, during which they sat on the floor amidst the boxes and shared a pizza, they resumed packing. Kayla's friend, Trish, arrived with her truck, and together they loaded up the items destined for a new home. Trish, a petite woman with a cheerful demeanor, and an enthusiasm that was contagious, chatted animatedly about her plans for the items, making the process feel less like an ending and more like a beginning.

By late afternoon, the house was completely packed except for an air mattress sitting in a corner of the living room. "You sure you don't want to spend the night at my place?" When Maxine nodded, Kayla promised to return early the next morning to help her wherever she could and to see her one last time before she left.

Closing the door behind her friend, Maxine leaned back against it and released a tired sigh. A slow smile spread across her face as she took in the boxes stacked everywhere. "I'm really doing this." Pushing away from the door, she walked over to the box that held the air mattress and knelt before ripping off the tape and opening the top.

Early the next morning, the movers arrived a few minutes before 8 am and Kayla arrived shortly after. Maxine directed the movers as they carefully loaded her belongings into the moving van. The sight of her life packed into boxes and stacked neatly in the truck was surreal. It was a tangible representation of the huge step she was taking.

As the last box was loaded, Maxine stood in the driveway, looking at the house she had called home for so long. Kayla came up beside her, placing a comforting hand on her shoulder. "You okay?" Her voice was soft with sadness.

Maxine nodded, blinking back tears. "Yeah, I think so. It's just... it's a lot, you know?"

"I know." Kayla gave her a reassuring smile and squeezed her shoulder. "But you're doing the right thing. This new place, this new adventure, it's exactly what you need."

Maxine took a deep breath and exhaled slowly, feeling a sense of calm wash over her. "You're right. It's time for a fresh start."

They stood in silence for a moment, watching the movers secure the last of the boxes in the truck. Finally, Maxine turned to Kayla with a determined smile. "Well, I guess that's it. Let's go inside and do one last walk-through."

Inside, the house felt eerily empty. The echo of their footsteps on the bare floors was a stark reminder of how much had changed. Maxine walked from room to room, memories flooding her mind with each step. The living room, where she'd hosted countless gatherings with friends. The kitchen, where she'd experimented with new recipes. Her bedroom, a sanctuary of solace during tough times.

As they reached the front door, Maxine turned to Kayla. "Thank you for everything, Kayla. I couldn't have done this without you."

Kayla smiled, her eyes glistening with unshed tears.

"Of course. That's what friends are for. And don't forget, I'm just a phone call away. Anytime you need anything, you call me."

Maxine hugged her tightly. "I will. And you better come visit me as soon as I'm settled in."

"You can count on it." Kayla wiped beneath her eyes as she hugged Maxine back just as tightly.

As they stepped outside, Maxine took one last look at her house before pulling the door closed and turning the key in the lock for the last time. Turning slightly, she held the key ring out to Kayla. "She's all yours."

Taking the key, Kayla spoke as she followed Maxine to her car. "I'll contact you as soon as we have a buyer."

"You better contact me before then." Opening the car door, she put one foot inside the car and blinked back tears as she stared at her friend. "Who knew leaving would be so hard?" When Kayla waved her off without speaking, she sat down in the driver's seat and pulled the door closed, lifting her hand in a final wave before starting the engine and dropping the gearshift into drive.

two

The drive to her new home was long but filled with anticipation. The winding roads took her through picturesque landscapes, each turn bringing her closer to her destination. She played her favorite music, singing along to keep her nerves at bay. The thought of starting over in a new town was both exhilarating and terrifying.

When she finally arrived at the cabin, she gasped and eased her foot down on the brake. Bringing her car to a stop, Maxine leaned forward and stared at the cabin in front of her before looking down at her GPS, which had rerouted her several times as she had made her way up the mountain road. Her heart sank as she looked from her GPS and back to the cabin. "This can't be right?" Reaching over, she opened the glove compartment and pulled out the images she had printed out the day Kayla had found the property listing, comparing them to the run-down cabin in front of her. Her eyes moved from the listing photos to the cabin and back again. The photos showed a charming cabin with a porch swing covered in pillows and flower boxes filled with greenery attached to the windows. The cabin in front of her looked nothing like the photos. The porch swing hung by one rusty chain on one side, while the other side rested against the porch floor. The flower boxes were non-existent and several panes in one window were shattered. A horn honked behind her, and her eyes shifted to the rearview mirror. Seeing the moving truck inching its way toward her, she took a deep breath and released it slowly, as nervous excitement flared to life inside her once again. Lifting her foot from the brake, she steered her car to the right and pulled forward, stopping again when she was beside the cabin. Turning the car off, she pushed her door open and stepped out, her chest expanding as she breathed in the cool mountain air before closing the door and making her way to the front of the cabin where the moving truck was backing in. Stepping up onto the porch, Maxine swallowed her trepidation and looked out across the mountain. The view before her almost made her forget the dilapidated state of the cabin. The surrounding forest blazed with fall colors; oranges, reds, and golds as far as the eye could see and a smile tugged gently at her lips as she leaned against the porch railing and closed her eyes, turning her face to the sky. As the movers stepped down from the truck, Maxine opened her eyes and stood in awe, once again taking in the beautiful view from her new home. She could already imagine herself sitting on the porch with a cup of coffee, watching the sunrise over the mountains in the mornings and the moon hanging between them at night. A smile curved her mouth as she took one more breath of fresh air before turning to unlock the cabin door.

Standing in the middle of the living room, surrounded by boxes and furniture, Maxine did her best to ignore the tiny voice in her head telling her that she had made a horrible mistake. The entire cabin needed to be swept, mopped, and the cabinets scoured before she could unpack. Her gaze traveled around the room, landing on the broken window. "Need to put something over that before night fall." Her voice sounded loud to her own ears, reminding her just how alone she was on top of Mirror Springs Mountain. Shaking the thought away, she picked up the box marked 'bedroom linens' and carried it down the hall to the bedroom that she had claimed as her own.

Stepping into the room, her eyes were instantly drawn to the floor-to-ceiling picture window that offered a breathtaking view of the mountains across the ridge. She smiled as she watched a large bird soaring over the tops of the trees, its wings stretched wide as it swooped and dipped before flying higher. Tearing her gaze away, she carried the box over to the dresser that the movers had left sitting haphazardly near the closet and set the box on top before turning her attention to the bed frame leaning against the plastic-wrapped mattress against the far wall. Reaching up, she gathered her hair into a high ponytail and secured it with the hair tie that she always wore on her wrist, before clapping her hands together and speaking softly to herself. "Okay Max, time to get to work." Heading out of the room, she hummed beneath her breath as she made her way to the kitchen in search of cleaning supplies.

The sun was high in the sky by the time Max finished cleaning enough to set up her bed. She had initially planned to just clean the bedroom but decided to clean the kitchen as well while she waited for the bedroom floor to dry. Pushing her fisted hands into the small of her back, she stretched as she walked down the short hallway to the bedroom again. Her gaze drifted back to the window for a fleeting second as she walked across the room and reached for the bed rails. She struggled with the pieces, her muscles straining as she lifted and maneuvered the heavy wooden headboard and footboard into position. Beads of sweat formed on her forehead, and she wiped them away with the back of her hand, her brow wrinkled in determination as she connected one of the metal rails to the footboard.

Hours passed as she worked tirelessly, not just on the bed but on unpacking and arranging her belongings, sweeping and mopping as she went. Each item found its place in the cabin, and with each piece she unpacked, the space began to feel more like home. She hung up pictures, arranged books on the shelves, and even set up a cozy reading nook by the window with a plush armchair and a soft blanket. Despite the exhaustion setting in, Maxine felt a sense of accomplishment as she took in the transformation of the cabin's interior.

Stepping from the cabin, she took a deep breath of the crisp mountain air and pulled her shawl around her shoulders. She smiled softly as she walked over to the porch swing that she had rehung earlier. Sitting down, she sighed tiredly before kicking the swing into motion as she cradled a cup of hot chocolate between her palms. Closing her eyes, she rolled her head from side to side, sighing again, this time with relief, when her neck popped. Opening her eyes, she took a drink from the cup and stared at the mountains across the valley. The sun had already set but there was still enough light left that she could enjoy the view from her front porch.

Lifting her cup to her lips again, she was taking a sip when a streak of lightning flashed over the mountains followed seconds later by a low rumble of thunder. Lowering the cup, she got to her feet and walked across the porch to lean against the railing as she watched the flashes of lightning, her nose twitching as the smell of fallen leaves decaying on the forest floor filled her senses. Earlier, as she was covering the broken window with a lawn-sized trash bag, she had once again questioned her decision to buy Mirror Springs Mountain and move into the old cabin, but now she knew she had made the right choice. Hearing a howl in the distance, she turned her head towards it and smiled again when several more wolves answered the first.

Pushing away from the railing, she made her way back to the front door and, after glancing around once more, stepped back inside the cabin.

Inside the cozy warmth of the cabin, she removed her shawl and hung it by the door. The wind began to howl, and a heavy rain pattered against the roof as the storm outside picked up. Maxine set her empty cup on the dining table and looked around the rustic kitchen, feeling a deep sense of peace settling over her.

She wandered through the cabin, her fingers trailing along the rough-hewn wooden walls. The place had a charm that the photos hadn't captured, an old-world feel that resonated with her. She found herself in the living room again, where boxes still littered the floor. She decided to tackle a few more before calling it a night.

Maxine pulled open a box labeled "kitchenware" and began to unpack plates, glasses, and utensils, carefully placing them in the cabinets and drawers. As she worked, memories of her decision to leave the city behind flickered in her mind. The stress, the noise, the constant rush—it all seemed so distant now. Here, she felt like she could breathe, like she could finally relax for the first time in months.

She was arranging a set of mugs on a shelf when a loud crash from the bedroom startled her. Heart racing, she grabbed a flashlight from the kitchen drawer and cautiously made her way down the hallway. The storm outside had intensified, and she could hear the wind whipping through the trees, making the cabin creak and groan.

Pushing the bedroom door open, she scanned the room with the flashlight. The footboard of the bed had fallen, and the foot of the mattress was sitting on the floor. Maxine sighed, frustration bubbling up inside her. She set the flashlight on the dresser and began to pull the covers from the mattress, her movements slow and deliberate as exhaustion weighed on her.

After reattaching the footboard, she replaced the mattress and remade the bed before changing into her pajamas and crawling beneath the covers. As exhausted as she was, Maxine lay in bed listening to the storm raging through the mountain. She watched shadows play across the ceiling each time lightning lit up the sky outside. Her heartbeat quickened with each silence-shattering boom of thunder, and she turned her head slightly to look out the window across the room. Earlier in the day, she had told herself that she had no need to hang curtains but now she questioned her reasoning.

Sitting up, she kept her eyes on the window as she got to her feet and slowly approached it. A flicker of orange light in the distance held her attention and she wondered if a tree had been struck by lightning. When the sky lit up again, she gasped and stepped to the side of the window as her heartbeat quickened again. She wondered if someone was out in the mountains and could see her standing at the window staring out.

Pushing away from the wall, she ran on tiptoe towards the door and jerked it open. She had a vague idea where the tote containing her curtains was and she hurried through the dark towards the front of the cabin. A startled cry left her lips when her right foot came down in something wet and she pinwheeled her arms to keep from falling. Her mouth opened in a silent scream when she lost her footing, and her left elbow slammed into the hardwood floor. Clutching her elbow with her right hand, she squeezed her eyes shut, her breath hitching in her throat as a tear rolled from the corner of her eye. This wasn't how she thought her first night in her new home would be, but here she was, lying on the floor, her arm possibly broken, her nightshirt soaked through at the back, and water dripping down on her from above.

Taking a deep breath, she opened her eyes and stared up at the ceiling above for several more minutes before rolling to her knees and cautiously getting to her feet. Walking slowly now, she made her way to the living room and felt along the wall for the light switch. As the room filled with light, she looked down at her injured elbow, doing her best to look at it without straightening her arm. She hissed in pain as she gingerly probed the area, the skin red and already starting to swell. Cradling her arm against her side, she looked around the room for the tote containing her curtains and spotted it sitting below three other totes marked canned goods. Groaning, she looked over her shoulder towards the bedroom before releasing a deep sigh and walking back to get her comforter and pillow.

On her way back out of the bedroom, she cast one last glance at the window before clutching her bedding to her chest with one arm and making her way back to the living room and the couch tucked beneath the window.

three

Fox took another sip from the steaming mug in his hand and stared across the valley between the two mountains towards the old cabin that, until yesterday, had sat vacant for over twenty years. He wondered if the rumors of a woman buying the mountain were true and chuckled as he shook his head when he saw smoke rising from the chimney. Taking another sip, he swallowed and looked at the watch on his wrist, sighing and tossing the rest of his coffee on the ground when he noted the time.

Turning back towards his tent, he let out a shrill whistle and chuckled when his brother groaned. "Time to get up, Jacob. We've got a long hike ahead of us if we want to reach Juniper's Ledge by noon. His brother's voice was muffled when he answered.

"Go on without me, Fox. It's too damn cold to be hiking anyway."

Turning, Fox walked over to his brother's tent and pulled the zipper up before grabbing hold of the flaps and throwing them open. Reaching in, he tugged on the sleeping bag Jacob was wrapped up in. "This was your idea, remember? Come on, man, get up. I took off work for this."

Sitting up, Jacob scrubbed at his face and took in a deep breath, snorting a bit as he did, before releasing it and glaring out the tent at Fox. "Please tell me there's coffee."

Fox pointed over his shoulder with his thumb as he straightened. "Hanging over the fire." Without waiting for a reply, he walked over to his own tent and pulled back the flaps, securing them before crawling inside to retrieve his backpack.

Jacob was looking up and following the flight path of a screeching hawk when his brother's phone began ringing for the third time. Sighing, he stopped walking and reached for his canteen. "You may as well go ahead and answer it."

Fox shook his head and held his hand out for the canteen. Taking a swig, he swallowed and passed it back before responding. "I took off today to go on this hike with you, that means no work for either one of us."

Nodding, Jacob inclined his head towards the phone clipped on Fox's hip as it continued to ring. "As much as I appreciate it, I'd enjoy the hike a hell of a lot more if I didn't have to keep listening to that."

Rolling his eyes, Fox unclipped his phone and looked at the caller ID before swiping to answer. "Yeah?"

"I'm sorry. I may have the wrong number. I'm trying to reach a Mr. Holton."

"You've reached one of them. How can I help you, Miss...?"

"Oh, sorry. My name is Maxine Prescott. I just moved to the area recently and I'm in need of a handyman. I found your number online and I was wondering if you are available for hire."

Fox looked back towards the way they had come, his gaze focused on the direction of where the cabin would be before he looked at his brother. "I'm a little tied up at the moment, but I have an opening for tomorrow. What sort of work are you needing to be done, Miss Prescott?"

Jacob's brow shot up as his eyes widened and he pointed over his shoulder with his thumb.

Nodding, Fox listened to the woman's snort of laughter on the other end of the phone call.

"Well, to start, the roof is leaking in the living room. And there's something funky going on with the plumbing."

"Funky, how?" Silence greeted his question, and he waved Jacob away when he leaned forward in an attempt to hear the conversation. "Ma'am? You still there?"

"Yes, sorry. Umm... well... there's this noise when I turn on the taps and it's really bad when I flush the toilet or use the shower."

It was his turn to snort. "Well, ma'am. Given that the cabin has been empty for nearly twenty - five years, I'm surprised you even have running water up there."

"You...? How do you know where I live? I didn't mention it."

"It's a small town, ma'am. You're the only person that's recently moved here in a while."

"Right. So... What time can I expect you tomorrow, Mr. Holton?"

Fox looked up at the sky for a second as he

mentally ran through his current projects. "I can be there around seven or seven thirty."

"In the morning?"

"Unless that's going to be a problem."

"No. No problem at all. The sooner the better. Thank you, Mr. Holton. I'll see you in the morning."

Pulling the phone away from his ear, Fox watched the small phone icon in the upper left corner blink off before he returned his phone to the holster on his side.

"So... you're going up there in the morning?"

Fox nodded and continued up the path that would lead them to Juniper's Ledge. "First thing in the morning. She's got roofing issues and a plumbing problem."

Jacob snorted before speaking. "At the very least. A cabin that old is bound to have serious structural damage and don't even get me started on the electrical. She's probably looking at a complete rebuild at the minimum."

Fox looked over in time to see his brother rubbing his hands together and smiling at the prospect of such a big job. "Let's not get ahead of ourselves, okay? Hell, we don't even know if she'll stick around that long. Especially if what you're saying turns out to be true." Grabbing the straps of his backpack, he shrugged it into a more comfortable position and began walking again. "We need to get going if we want to get there and back before nightfall."

Jacob was silent for a second before speaking as he looked up at the sky again. "We'll need to take the shortcut back to the bottom of the mountain, so we don't have to spend the night again. Don't want to be late in the morning, right?"

Fox nodded in agreement and walked a little faster.

The trail to Juniper's Ledge was narrow and steep, winding through the dense forest and rocky outcrops. Fox and Jacob hiked in silence for a while, the only sounds were the crunch of their boots on the ground and the occasional call of a bird. The air was crisp and fresh, carrying the earthy scent of pine and damp leaves.

As they climbed higher, the trees thinned, and the view opened up, revealing the vast expanse of the valley below. Fox paused to catch his breath, leaning on his hiking pole, and took in the sight. Turning slightly, he looked back the way they had come. The cabin was just a speck from this distance, smoke still curling lazily from the chimney.

"Beautiful, isn't it?" Jacob lifted his camera and snapped a few photos as he came to a stop beside his brother.

Fox nodded, a smile tugging at his lips. "Yeah, it is. Makes you forget all about the world down there."

They continued their ascent, the path becoming more challenging as they neared the ledge. Fox's muscles burned with exertion, but he relished the physical challenge. It reminded him of why he loved hiking and being in nature, away from the noise and stress of everyday life.

By the time they reached Juniper's Ledge, the sun was high in the sky, casting long shadows across the rocky outcrop. They dropped their packs and sat on the edge, legs dangling over the side as they took in the panoramic view.

"This was a good idea." Jacob smiled over at Fox and wiped the sweat from his brow. "Thanks for coming with me today."

Fox grinned and clapped him on the back. "Anytime, brother. Anytime."

They spent the next hour resting and exploring the ledge, snapping photos and marveling at the sheer drop-off on the other side. The ledge provided a perfect vantage point to see the surrounding mountains; their peaks dusted with early snow.

As the afternoon wore on, Fox glanced at his watch and stood up. "We should start heading back if we want to make it back to the truck before dark."

Jacob nodded, reluctantly pulling his pack back on. "Yeah, you're right. Can't keep Miss Prescott waiting."

They made their way down the mountain, taking the shortcut Jacob had suggested. The path was steep and treacherous in places, requiring them to use both hands and feet to navigate the rocky terrain as they descended. Fox's thoughts wandered to the woman waiting at the cabin. He wondered what she was like and what had prompted her to buy such a remote, rundown place.

The sun was setting by the time they reached their campsite, casting a golden glow over the landscape. They packed up quickly, stowing their gear and making sure they hadn't left any trash on the ground before setting off again. The last stretch of the hike was done in the gathering dusk, the forest growing dark and silent around them.

When they finally emerged onto the road where

the truck was parked, Fox let out a tired breath. "Freaking finally."

Chuckling, Jacob slapped him on the back. "This was a great day, wasn't it? Now let's get home and get some rest. We've got a big day tomorrow."

four

Maxine drummed her fingers on the kitchen counter and checked the time on her phone for the fifth time before glancing longingly at the coffee maker. Mr. Holton wasn't due to arrive for at least another thirty minutes and she berated herself for not filling the machine with water before going to bed last night. Rubbing her forehead with the back of her hand, she was walking towards the living room when she heard a door slam outside. Hurrying towards the door, she pulled it open and caught her breath as she slowly leaned back to stare up at the tall man standing in front of her, his fisted hand raised poised to knock. He wasn't anything like what she had been expecting. Well over six feet tall, his hair was jet black and his long black lashes framed eyes so light blue they could almost pass for a frosty white. Releasing her breath, she smiled up at him as she reached up to push a stray lock of hair over her ear. "He... hello. Mr. Holton?"

Fox stared down at her and nodded once, slowly, his gaze quickly taking in her wild mane of brown hair, her piercing green eyes, and the dimples on each side of her mouth when she smiled. "Sorry, I'm a little early. I can wait out in..."

"No." When his eyes widened, she huffed out a slight chuckle and stepped back to wave him in. "What I mean is, if you can come in and take a look at the plumbing in the kitchen, that would be fantastic. I had water when I went to bed, but when I got up this morning there was no water."

Nodding as she spoke, Fox watched her nervously tugging the ends of a strand of hair that had fallen over her left shoulder. He briefly wondered if it felt as soft as it looked and curled his hand into a tight fist to keep from reaching out to touch it. When he realized she was no longer speaking, he cleared his throat and met her gaze again. "Is it just the kitchen or...?"

She was shaking her head before he could finish, oblivious to the way his eyes kept straying to her hair. Waving towards the inside of the cabin, she turned slightly and looked over her shoulder. "It's the entire cabin, actually."

Fox arched an eyebrow as he stepped past her and looked towards the kitchen. "The entire cabin?"

Closing the door, Maxine rubbed her hands together nervously and nodded. "I'm really hoping it's something minor, but I fear it may be a busted pipe. I don't have any tools, or I'd try to fix the damned thing myself."

Fox held up a finger for silence and tilted his head to the left. After a few minutes, he nodded and turned back to the front door. "I think you're right about that busted pipe. I'll need to turn it off at the main valve before I can fix it. Shouldn't take long to fix but, you'll want to give it a few hours for the glue to cure before I can turn the water back on."

"A few hours? But..." Her gaze strayed to the cup in his hand before she raised her eyes to meet his again. "I'll need to go into town to pick up a few cases of water. Would you mind if I left you here alone, Mr. Holton?"

"Please call me Ryder or Fox, Miss Prescott. I don't mind at all, but are you sure you're okay leaving me here alone?"

Maxine waved his words away as she turned towards the hallway, her hair bouncing with the movement. "I'm sure. And you may as well call me Maxine or Max, either is fine." Stopping, she turned to face him and gave him a lopsided smile. "I'm going to get my things while you turn the water off and I'll be out in a minute. If I need to get anything in town to help with the repairs, just write it down and I'll pick it up. There's paper and a pen on the kitchen table." Without waiting for his reply, she walked into her room and closed the door behind her.

Fox stared at the closed bedroom door for a moment, then shook his head as a slight smile turned his lips up at the corners. Walking back outside, he got his tools from the back of the truck and made his way to the side of the house where the main water valve was located. As he worked, his mind wondered to the woman he had just met. Maxine Prescott was nothing like he expected her to be. Word around town was she had moved to Mirror Springs Mountain from New York City and some of the locals were taking bets on how long she'd last before tucking tail and scurrying back to the "Big Apple". After his brief encounter with her, he had a feeling she wasn't the type of woman to give up so easily.

After shutting the water off, he carried his tools with him as he went back inside the cabin. Turning his attention to the kitchen, Fox set his tool bag down and pulled a pad of paper from his back pocket, flipping it open with his thumb as he walked over to the kitchen sink and looked out the window. Watching a squirrel scratching at the ground beneath a tree, he plucked a pen from his shirt pocket and dropped his gaze to the pad as he wrote down his business address and Jacob's number. He was tearing the paper free when he heard a door open down the hallway seconds before Max spoke.

"I shouldn't be gone very long, and I'll bring back something for breakfast if you're hungry. You have any food allergies I should be aware of?"

Fox's mouth curved up at the corner as he watched her fussing with her hair. "No ma'am, but you don't have to feed me. I'm fine, really."

Max waved his words away. "You're right, I don't but I want to, especially if you'll be here for several hours." Seeing the paper in his hand, she reached towards him. "Is that your list?"

Shaking his head, Fox let her take the paper from his hand. "That is the address to my shop along with my brother's number."

Max arched an eyebrow as she glanced up from the paper. "Your brother?"

Fox dipped his head in a brief nod. "He's my business partner. I'll give him a call to let him know you'll be stopping by to pick up what I need but, if he's not there when you arrive, you can call him to let him know you're in town."

Folding the paper, she slid it into the front pocket of her cargo pants and turned towards the door. "I'll be back as quick as I can. There's soda in the fridge if you get thirsty before I return." Lifting her keys from a hook by the front door, she looked back at him and gave him a terse smile before pulling the door open and stepping from the cabin.

five

Pulling to a stop in front of the local diner, Max shifted her car into park before opening the glove compartment and retrieving her wallet. Unzipping it, she pulled out her spare cash before returning the wallet to the glove compartment and pushing it closed again. Removing the keys from the ignition switch, she reached over and locked the glove compartment before opening the driver's side door and stepping out into the early morning breeze. Closing the door absently, she let her gaze travel over the front of the quaint diner, a small smile toying with the corners of her mouth, and she pressed the lock button on her key fob twice as she breathed in the scent of bacon mingled with the crisp fall air. With a contented sigh, she looked around the town square as she made her way to the entrance of the diner, her boot heels clicking softly against the sidewalk. As she reached for the door handle, she noticed a whiteboard propped in the window near the door:

"Today's special: Homemade Chili, served with a slice of freshly baked cornbread and pumpkin pie for dessert."

Max smiled as her stomach rumbled. Pushing the door open, she stepped into the warmth of the diner's interior and made her way across the room as the aroma of freshly brewed coffee filled her senses.

"Good morning, missy. What can I get 'cha?"

Max gave the waitress a warm smile and pointed towards the coffee pot. "Can I get a cup of coffee, please?"

Pulling a notepad from her apron pocket, the waitress removed a pencil from behind her ear and started writing. "Sugar? Cream?"

"Both. Heavy on the cream. And I'd also like to order two of the house specials, but I'll be back later to pick it up if that's okay." Max blushed when her stomach rumbled again.

Smiling, the waitress scribbled as she spoke. "Sure thing, sugar. You want that coffee for here or to go?"

Max looked towards an empty booth near the window in the back before speaking. "Here." Looking back at the waitress, she pointed at the booth. "Is that booth reserved?"

Chuckling, the waitress reached for a large mug before picking up the coffee decanter. "No reservations needed around here, missy. Sit wherever you please and I'll bring your coffee to you if you'd like."

Max shook her head and reached towards the mug. "I'll take that now, but I would like to order some breakfast."

"The special this morning is crispy bacon, eggs cooked your way, fried potatoes with onions, creamy gravy, and buttermilk biscuits. We serve the gravy on the side or on top of your biscuits, whichever you please." She held her pencil poised over the top of the notepad as she waited for Max to speak.

Max ran her thumb over her top lip before speaking. "I'll take two of the breakfast specials, but one will be to go. I'm not sure how Mr. Holten likes his eggs or gravy, but I'll have the eggs scrambled and the gravy on the side."

The waitress raised an eyebrow as she looked up from her pad. "Fox or Jacob?"

Max lowered the cup and swallowed before replying. "Oh, umm, Fox."

The waitress pointed her pencil in Max's direction and gave her a wink. "Got 'cha. I'll get this to the cook and bring it out shortly. I'll box Fox's breakfast up with your lunch specials and have them waiting for you when you get back."

"Thank you." When the waitress turned away, Max walked towards the back of the diner and made her way to the empty booth, her mug of coffee cradled between her palms.

Sliding into the booth, she sipped her coffee and sat back as she allowed herself to relax for the first time since arriving, the soft hum of conversation and the clinking of silverware scraping glass dishes filling the air. Turning her head, she studied the buildings around the square, her eyes stopping as she spotted the sign above the awning of the building down the street: "Holton's Home Remodel and Services." Lost in her thoughts, she was startled when she felt a tap on her shoulder. Looking up, she leaned away from the man standing too close and waved her fingers at him. "Could you kindly back up, please?" She resisted the urge to lift her top lip in annoyance when he chuckled before taking a dramatic step back.

Removing his hat, he bowed and spoke mockingly. "My sincerest apologies, ma'am."

Narrowing her eyes, she let her gaze travel over him, noting his stained jeans with the knees ripped and his worn leather jacket, before speaking. "Can I help you in some way?"

Standing straight, he put his hat back on before extending his hand in her direction. "Jacob Holton, ma'am. And you'd be Maxine Prescott, the lady that bought Mirror Springs Mountain out from under me."

Max's eyes widened and she flattened a palm against her chest. "I beg your pardon?"

Waving her words away, he laughed as he slid into the booth across from her. "I'm just messing with you, ma'am. It's part of my charm."

Max arched an eyebrow at him. "You think you're charming?"

Jacob gasped in mock shock. "Are you saying I'm not? I am offended. Truly I am. Hurt down to my core."

Max fought down a smile as she cleared her throat and took another sip from her mug. Lowering the mug to the table, she waited for him to speak and released a sigh when he continued to stare at her. "You wanna tell me what you need, or do you plan to keep me in suspense?"

Raising his hand, he motioned to get the waitress's attention and pointed at Max's cup when she looked over at them. Turning back to face her, he smiled before speaking. "Fox told me to gather up some supplies for you to pick up on your way out of town and I figured I'd hitch a ride back to your place with you."

"Hitch a ride? With me?"

Looking up at the waitress, he accepted his mug and winked at her. "Thanks, darling."

Rolling her eyes, she shook her head and walked away mumbling about insolent man-boys.

"I think you've upset our hostess."

Jacob looked over his shoulder before facing Max again. "Nah. Darlene pretends to hate it when I call her darling, but she ignores me if I call her anything else." When Max gave him a skeptical look, he wrapped his hands around his coffee mug and leaned forward, dropping the pitch of his voice low. "She was my older sister's best friend in school and, being a brat at the age of twelve, I started calling her darling as a joke. It just kinda stuck, ya know?"

She wanted to ask why he said 'was' but quickly decided it wasn't any of her business and brought the subject back around to their previous conversation. "So, why can't you drive yourself up to Mirror Springs Mountain?"

"I could, but since you're already going that way and my brother is already there, it seems like a pretty resourceful option to ride there with you." He looked up again when Darlene stopped at the table with Max's breakfast.

"Don't believe anything this one tells you, missy. He's a charmer, this one." Setting the plate and bowl of gravy down in front of Max, she straightened and pointed at Jacob. "You want anything besides coffee, Jay?"

Jacob shook his head. "Not this morning. I might be back in this evening for some of that chili though."

"I'll tell Billy to make it the way you like it. If you don't come back in, I'll drop it off on my way home tonight." As she was walking away, she stopped and turned back to him. "Tell Shelly I'll be round Sunday to pick her up for church."

Jacob sighed and looked down at his cup. "Will do."

Max looked from Darlene's crestfallen face back to Jacob's bowed head and couldn't hold back her questions. "What did I just witness? Is Shelly your wife?"

Jacob was silent for several seconds before he lifted

his head and shook it. "Shelly is my older sister and Darlene has been trying to get her out of the house for the past fifteen years." When Max's eyes widened, he continued. "When they were seniors in high school, they took off for their senior day of freedom. A bunch of their friends went in one car and Darlene and Shelly took Shelly's truck. I'm not really sure about the full details, but the car in front of them spun out and Shelly didn't break in time. Shelly was trapped in the truck, and it was on fire and..."

Max held up a hand to stop his next words. "You don't have to go into details." When he nodded and dropped his gaze to his mug, she released a pent-up breath and picked up her fork before laying it down again. "I'm sorry, I didn't mean to be rude. I just..."

"You don't have to apologize. I didn't think you were being rude. I should apologize for ruining your breakfast." Reaching forward, he swiped a piece of her bacon and looked at her for approval before dipping it in the bowl of gravy and putting the whole slice in his mouth.

Picking her fork back up, she stabbed at her eggs before scooping up some of the potatoes and taking a bite. She moaned as the savory flavor of the potatoes and the buttery flavor of the eggs mingled together on her tongue. Swallowing, she met Jacob's gaze as she forked up another bite and held it out to him. "You've gotta try this."

Leaning forward, Jacob closed his mouth around the fork and winked at her before sitting back, his mouth moving slowly as he chewed.

A blush stained Max's cheeks as she watched him before lowering her gaze back to her plate and using the fork to push her food around as she spoke. "I need to go to the store and pick up a few things, but I can meet you at your office when I'm done."

"Sounds good. I really appreciate..." His words trailed off when his phone chimed. Pulling it from the holster on his hip, he read the text and slid from the booth. "I won't be needing that ride after all." Pulling his wallet from his pocket, he tossed a few bills on the table and spoke as he put his wallet back in his pocket. "Honey will meet you at the office and help you load up Fox's supplies."

"Honey? Is that another pet name or...?"

Chuckling, he turned to leave, speaking over his shoulder. "That's her actual name. It was nice to meet you, Miss Prescott."

"You too." Max watched him walk out the door and couldn't resist watching him as he jogged down the street towards his office building.

"That man is always rushing off somewhere. I

swear he never slows down for more than a few minutes." Picking up his half-full mug, Darlene scooped up the money and glanced out the window in Jacob's direction once before walking away.

Max stared out the window a few seconds longer before returning her attention to her breakfast, ignoring her phone as it vibrated in her pocket.

six

Pulling a rag from his back pocket, Fox wiped his hands before flipping the switch on the hood vent above the cookstove and smiling in satisfaction when the fan kicked on. Turning away from the stove, he walked to the kitchen table and picked up his pencil before scratching through the words on his notepad: "Vent above the stove". Laying the pencil back down, he rubbed the back of his neck as he looked towards the living room. His mouth twitched up at the corner when he noticed the thin blanket covering the window. Glancing around at the pile of moving boxes and totes that still littered the room, his gaze stopped on the box marked "front room linens and throw pillows".

Looking down at his watch, he noted the time before going to the pile of boxes and moving them around until he reached the one he needed. Lifting it, he carried it over to the couch and ripped off the tape before opening the box and peering inside. The scent of vanilla and something spicy greeted him as he pulled a throw pillow from the box. Bringing it to his nose, he sniffed it again before placing it on the sofa. Reaching back into the box, he removed the matching pillow and the stack of maroon-colored curtains that was beneath it. Setting the pillow down next to the other one, he looked at the curtains and then looked up at the top of the window, hoping to see a curtain rod. When he didn't see one, he turned back to the box and pushed the rest of the linens around until his hand touched something metal in the corner of the box. Grasping it, he began to pull it but stopped when he heard a ripping sound. "What in the world?" Squinting down into the shadowy interior of the box, he ran his finger up the side of the metal rod until he felt the tape that was holding it in place. Curious, he checked each corner of the box and found three more metal rods taped into the corners of the box. Removing the tape from one of the rods, he pulled it from the box and smiled to himself when he saw the brackets securely taped to the side of the rod.

Getting to his feet, he went into the kitchen to

retrieve a screwdriver before going back into the living room and taking the blanket down from the window.

Max's heart swelled with appreciation as she stepped into the cabin, her eyes immediately drawn to the silk curtains now hanging over the living room window. The soft glow of mid-morning sunlight filtering through the fabric bathed the room in a warm, inviting light. With a soft smile, she made a mental note to thank Fox as she made her way into the kitchen. Setting the box containing their lunch and his breakfast on the seat of a dining room chair, she began to carefully arrange the carryout containers on the table, her mind preoccupied with renovation plans that she wanted to discuss with Fox.

"Where do you want these?"

Throwing a look over her shoulder, she saw Fox holding a bag of groceries in each arm. "On the counter will be fine. You really don't have to help unload the car."

"It's no big deal, really. I'm free until the pipes are ready to test anyway." Setting the bags down, he started back towards the front door. "I thought Jacob was going to hitch a ride with you?"

Max nodded and absently wiped her hands on the back of her jeans as she followed him from the cabin. "He was, but something came up."

"Did he happen to tell you what that something was?"

"Nope, and I didn't ask if you want the truth. Didn't think it was any of my business." Leaning into the car, she lifted a case of water and turned at the waist when Fox tried to take it from her. "I got this. But I wouldn't mind if you helped with the other three cases that are in the trunk." Without waiting for him to reply, she carried the case of water towards the cabin. As she stepped up onto the porch, her eyes were drawn to the woods across the open field. Stopping in her tracks, she gasped as she watched a black bear step into view, its nose lifted towards the sky.

"Don't be afraid. That's old Jasmine. She won't hurt you as long as you don't try to mess with her cubs."

"Her cubs?" Max studied the area near the bear and slightly shook her head. "I don't see any cubs."

Stepping around her, Fox continued into the cabin. "That's because she won't have them until the winter when she's denned up. Right now, she's looking for food so she can gain her winter weight before she hibernates."

Max's head snapped in his direction, her eyes wide with fright. "Food? Is she... is the smell of our food going to bring her here?"

Placing the water on the floor by the fridge, he turned back to face her. "Jasmine has never shown aggression towards humans, so I don't think she will try to come into your cabin."

Max looked from the bear to Fox and back again. "How can you be sure that is Jasmine?"

Walking back to the front porch, he took the case of water from her and looked across the field at the bear. "You see that orange tag on her ear?" When Max nodded, he continued. "Jasmine was rescued a few years back from a trap and she was tagged before being released back into the wild."

Following him into the cabin, she hugged herself as her body began to tremble. "I didn't realize bears would be so close to the cabin."

Fox turned slowly to face her, his eyebrow arched in question. "You knew bears lived in these mountains, right?"

"I mean, I figured as much, I just didn't think they'd be right here in my own backyard." When Fox began to laugh, she huffed and glared up at him. "Are you laughing at me?"

"I'm sorry, really, but this whole mountain range is your backyard now, even the parts you didn't buy. There are more bears besides Jasmine in this area, as well as mountain lions, bobcats, boars... You name it, it's most likely lurking somewhere close." When she looked back over her shoulder towards the open cabin door, Fox cleared his throat and bit the inside of his cheek to keep from laughing again. "When I come back tomorrow, I'll bring you an air horn and some bear spray."

Nodding absently, she walked over to the door and gently pushed it closed. Turning back to face him, she dipped her head towards the food containers on the table. "I brought you back some breakfast. I didn't know what you'd want, but Darlene seemed to know."

Fox looked up from the case of water he was opening and dipped his head in a slight nod. "Thank you."

Returning his nod, she looked towards the curtained window before pushing away from the door. "I'm going to go sort out the guest room. If you need me..." She let her words trail off when he nodded again, his cheeks bulged out from the bite of biscuit and gravy he had just put in his mouth. Smothering a smile, she walked from the room and made her way to the guest room.

Max leaned against the kitchen counter and stared out at Fox as he removed the covering over the water valve. She waited until he gave her a thumbs up before turning on the water tap and whooping when water rushed from the faucet. Her joy was quickly replaced with concern when the water faucet began jumping and sputtering. Reaching forward, she quickly turned the tap off before knocking rapidly on the kitchen window to get Fox's attention. When he looked at her, she motioned for him to come inside. As he stepped inside a few minutes later, she gestured towards the sink. "I don't know what's wrong, but it started sputtering so hard the faucet was jumping."

Scratching his ear, Fox turned away and swallowed down his amusement. When he was sure he could speak without laughing, he faced her again and cleared his throat before replying. "There's air in the lines, so you'll need to let the water run until it clears. I'll go turn on the water in the bathroom."

Max waited until she was sure he couldn't see her before smacking her forehead with her palm and shaking her head. "Get it together Prescott. You're not this ditzy." Going back to the sink, she turned the water back on and stood back to watch as she waited for the air to clear the lines.

Fox spoke as he walked back into the room a few minutes later. "Bathroom is cleared. Oh, by the way, I found the roof leak while you were in town. The storm blew a few of the shingles up so I nailed them back down for the time being. There may be more damage up there, so I'll bring some replacement shingles out tomorrow when I come back." Glancing at his watch, he looked at the fridge, where she had placed the chili and cornbread earlier, longingly before sighing. "Well, I guess that'll do it for today."

Max turned to face him. "Wait, you're not leaving yet, are you?"

Fox dipped his head in a curt nod. "Unless there's something else that can't wait until tomorrow."

Shaking her head, Max washed her hands before opening the refrigerator door and pulling out the food she had brought back from the diner. "We haven't eaten yet and there's no way I can eat all of this by myself. Let me heat this up and we'll eat before you go."

"You don't have to…"

Max interrupted him. "You've said that already. Wash up and set the table. The plates are in the cabinet to the right of the stove and the silverware is in the top drawer by the sink."

Fox opened his mouth to protest but snapped it closed when she leveled a stern look in his direction. Giving her a mock salute, he snapped the heels of his boots together and stood tall, his eyes focused on a spot above her head. "Yes, ma'am."

Rolling her eyes, Max turned back to the stove and retrieved a pot from the lower cabinet to the left of the stove. "Just like your brother with the wisecracks, I see."

Fox chuckled next to her. "Where do you think he learned it?" When she cut her eyes at him, he laughed a bit louder as he pulled down two soup bowls and two small plates. "If you have a convection oven, I can set it up and get the cornbread into heat."

Max pointed over her shoulder with her thumb. "It's in one of those boxes in the living room if you feel like digging for it."

Fox looked at the mountain of boxes before looking back at Max. "How about I bring the ones marked 'kitchen' in here and unpack them while you get that heated up?"

Max released an unladylike snort before turning to look at him. "This will be cold again before you can finish unpacking all those boxes. May as well eat while it's hot and then, if you're still feeling helpful, we can unpack them together."

"Deal." Turning towards the living room, Fox laced his fingers together and cracked his knuckles playfully before stepping forward and walking towards the pile of moving boxes.

SEVEN

Rolling over in bed, Max's gaze drifted to the bedroom window. Her ears rang with the silence of the night, punctuated by the occasional distant howl of a wolf or coyote. Sighing, she threw back the covers, shivering as the frigid air in the room brushed across her skin. The wooden floorboards creaked beneath her bare feet when she stood. Teeth chattering from the cold, she rubbed her arms briskly as she shuffled across the room to the window and opened the curtains before hurrying back to bed. Pulling the covers up to her chin, she curled into herself as she looked out the window at the stars twinkling high above the tree line. She'd always hated the silence of the night but, living in isolation, the silence was almost more than she could bear. She longed for the sounds of the city, the distant laughter of couples as they walked along the sidewalk outside her old house. The honking of horns when traffic was stalled. She missed her old life more than ever tonight and she couldn't understand why. Rolling over, so that her back faced the window, she grabbed the extra pillow and pulled it up to cover her head, praying that sleep would take her soon.

Sleep flirted with her, offering a brief moment of escape, only to be snatched away by a strange sound from outside her window. A snort, low and guttural, filled the room. Sitting up, her heart began to race as visions of the bear flitted through her mind. The moon cast shadows across the far wall, and she held her breath as she watched one of them move slowly to the left. Turning to look over her shoulder, she debated going to the window but changed her mind when the snort came again, louder and closer.

Her panicked thoughts screamed at her to run and hide, but she remained where she was, her eyes glued to the window as she listened to the sounds coming from outside. Her breath hitched in her throat, and she covered her mouth with a trembling hand as something thudded against the side of the cabin near the front door. Springing into action, she jumped from the bed and ran on tiptoe to the kitchen. Pulling a large knife from the butcher block, she held it up near her face as she moved silently to the window over-looking the porch. Easing the curtain to the side with one finger, she peeked out the window and breathed out a relieved laugh when she saw four small piglets chasing each other across the porch, their tiny bodies illuminated by the solar-powered lanterns Fox had hung on each end of the porch for her the day before. Lowering the knife, she stood at the window watching them play until movement from the corner of her eye caught her attention. Looking to her left, her breath caught again when a large pig stepped from the shadows and looked towards the porch, its eyes glinting in the lantern light. A loud squeal ripped through the frigid mountain air, instantly bringing the piglets' play to an end. Max watched as they trotted to the edge of the porch and hopped down before running over to the larger pig, releasing tiny squeals and snorts as they followed it across the open field. Max watched them fade from her line of sight before releasing the curtain, her smile fading as she looked down at the knife in her hand. Turning, she was walking towards the kitchen to return the knife but changed her mind and carried it with her as she made her way down the hall and back to her bedroom. Walking over to the window, she was about to close the curtain when the faint glow of a campfire across the ridge caught her attention. She made a mental note to ask Fox about it in the morning as she pulled the curtains over the window and retreated back across the room, laying the knife on the bedside table before getting back into bed. Shivering against the cold, she listened to the rustle of leaves blowing across the yard outside until she finally drifted off to sleep.

Morning sunlight streamed through the gaps in the curtains, waking Max when they crept across the bed, reaching her closed lids. She stretched, a smile playing with her lips before releasing a contented sigh and rolling out of bed, her breath visible in the chilly air. The sight of the knife on the bedside table reminded her of the night before, and she chuckled to herself as she walked to her closet and pulled open the door, her gaze dropping to the boxes that still held her clothes. She dressed quickly, pulling on layers to ward off the cold, and made her way to the kitchen, the knife clutched in her hand. Laying the knife in the sink, she lifted the coffee carafe and placed it beneath the faucet before turning the water on. When the carafe was full, she poured the water into the coffee pot, added a filter pack, and pressed the start button. While she waited for the coffee to brew, she dragged one of the boxes filled with canned goods over to the pantry and began to unpack it.

Ten minutes later, she stepped out onto the porch, a steaming mug of coffee cradled between her palms. Max inhaled deeply, savoring the crisp, clean air. The memory of the piglets playing brought a smile to her face, and she glanced towards the field where they had disappeared. There was no sign of them now, but she could still see their tiny hoof prints in the frost-covered grass.

The sound of an engine drew her attention, and she turned to see Fox's truck coming up the mountain road. She waved as he pulled to a stop and climbed out, his breath misting in the cold morning air.

"Morning, Max." Closing the truck door, he reached into the back of his truck and lifted out a box before turning to face her again. "How'd you sleep?"

"Better than I expected." Stepping down from the porch, Max smiled and squinted up at the sky as she continued. "Had a bit of excitement last night, though."

Fox raised an eyebrow. "Oh yeah? What happened?"

Max recounted the story of the piglets and the large pig, laughing as she described her initial fear and subsequent relief.

Fox chuckled, shaking his head. "Sounds like the Baker family's pigs. They've got a habit of wandering off. I'll give them a call and let them know their pigs paid you a visit."

"Thanks, Fox." Feeling a warm flush despite the cold, Max took a sip of her coffee and swallowed before speaking again. "By the way, I noticed a campfire on the ridge last night. Do you know anything about that?"

Fox's expression grew thoughtful. "Probably just some hikers or campers. That spot's popular for its view. I'll check it out later to make sure everything's alright."

Max nodded, feeling reassured. "Appreciate it. So, where do we start today?"

Fox glanced around, assessing the cabin's condition. "We'll tackle the roof first. Looks like it's seen better days."

They worked side by side, removing damaged shingles and inspecting the underlying structure before moving on to the next section. Max was grateful for Fox's expertise and patience as he explained each step of the process. The physical labor was a welcome distraction from her thoughts, and she found herself enjoying the rhythm of the work.

As they worked, they chatted about their lives. Max shared stories of her city life, the bustling energy of the streets, and the noise she once found comforting. Fox, in turn, spoke of his love for the mountains, the peace and solitude they offered, and the sense of connection he felt to the land.

"I guess we're opposites in that way." Max shrugged as she handed Fox another shingle. "You find peace in the silence, while I miss the noise."

Fox smiled. "It's all about perspective. The mountains have a different kind of noise. You just have to listen for it."

By midday, they had made significant progress on the roof. Fox called for a break, and they sat on the porch, drinking hot coffee and eating donuts Fox had brought with him.

"What's next on the list?" Max wiped her fingers on the legs of her pants before finishing her cup of coffee.

"I'd like to check the plumbing again." Setting his cup on the little table beside the porch swing, Fox stood and waited for her to get to her feet. "Did you have any issues after I left yesterday?"

Max nodded. "That same funky noise as the first day I was here." Leading him inside to the bathroom, she turned on the tap, and the familiar gurgling and clanking filled the room.

Fox knelt, examining the pipes. "Old pipes can be tricky. Sounds like there's air trapped in the lines again, maybe some blockages. We'll have to flush the system."

Max watched as he worked, feeling a mix of curiosity and admiration. Fox moved with confidence, his hands sure and steady as he adjusted valves and tapped on pipes.

Kneeling beside him, Max handed him a crescent wrench and spoke after he took it. "You really know your stuff, don't you?"

Fox shrugged modestly. "Just picked it up over the years. Living out here, you learn to be a jack-of-all-trades."

As he continued working, Max found herself drawn to his quiet demeaner. Something was reassuring about his presence, a steadiness that contrasted sharply with the uncertainty she often felt.

"Why did you decide to move out here, Max?" Glancing up from his work, Fox held her gaze, waiting for her to answer.

The question caught her off guard, and she hesitated, unsure how to answer. "I needed a change." Dropping her gaze, she avoided looking at him as the lie fell from her lips. "My life in the city... it just wasn't fulfilling anymore. I thought coming here might help me find... something."

Fox nodded, his expression thoughtful. "Sometimes a change of scenery is just what you need. These mountains have a way of showing you what's important."

Max pondered his words as she watched him work, wondering if she would find what she was looking for in this remote cabin.

By late afternoon, the plumbing issues were resolved, and together they had patched up the worst of the leaks in the roof. They stood in the living room, surveying their progress with satisfaction.

Giving her a warm smile, Fox nudged her playfully with his elbow. "You did great today. This place is already looking better."

Max beamed, feeling a sense of pride. "Couldn't have done it without you."

Fox packed up his tools, preparing to leave. "I'll be back tomorrow to finish up the roof and check on the electrical. If you need anything, don't hesitate to call."

Max walked him to the door, a sense of gratitude welling up inside her. "Thanks, Fox. For everything."

He tipped his hat and smiled. "Anytime, Max. See you tomorrow."

As she watched him drive away, Max felt a glimmer of hope. The cabin still needed a lot of work, but for the first time since she arrived, she felt like she was making progress. Trying to ignore the tingling in her lower stomach as she watched Fox's truck disappear around a bend in the mountain road, she closed the door and turned the lock before reaching up and releasing her hair as she made her way to the bathroom.

That night, as she lay in bed, the sounds of the forest outside felt less intimidating, more familiar. The memory of Fox's steady presence comforted her, and she found herself looking forward to the next day's work. The silence of the mountains was still a challenge, but it was one she was beginning to embrace.

eight

Holding a takeout cup of coffee in each hand, Fox looked at his watch before dipping his head towards the door, indicating that Jacob should knock again.

Knocking louder, Jacob looked over his shoulder at his brother and spoke in a slightly raised voice. "Maybe she's not here, man."

Fox pointed at her car with his pinky finger as he spoke. "She's got to be around here somewhere. Her car is still here, and she knows I was coming back this morning. She wouldn't just leave without..." His words trailed off as the cabin door swung open and a half-asleep Max squinted out at them, her hair sleep-tangled and sticking up on the right side of her head. "Uh... good morning?"

"You're early." Blinking slowly, Max covered a yawn with the crook of her elbow before dipping her head at the cups he was clutching. "One of those for me?"

Smiling brightly, Jacob took one of the cups from his brother and cheerfully held it out towards Max. "Your morning elixir, madam."

Yawning she reached for the cup and took a healthy drink before lowering it and looking back at Fox. "He always so chipper in the mornings?"

Fox cut his eyes towards Jacob and shook his head. "Usually he's a grouch and he never shares his coffee with anyone."

Max froze mid-sip, her wide-eyed stare darting from one brother to the next. She debated giving Jacob his coffee back before shrugging nonchalantly and taking another drink. Smacking her lips, she smiled up at Jacob and tipped the cup in his direction. "Thanks so much for sharing." Stepping back, she held the door open wider and motioned for them to enter. Once they were inside, she closed the door and moved towards the hallway. "If you will excuse me, I'll be right back." Shivering, she wrapped her arms over her chest as she walked down the hallway towards her room.

Jacob watched her until she disappeared into a

room down the hall before turning to face Fox and pointing over his shoulder with his thumb toward the door. "I think I'll go hunt up some wood and get a fire going. Might need to tell her about ol' Hollis so she can order a few ricks of wood to get her through this cold snap."

Fox nodded once and looked around the living room. "I'll get the fireplace cleaned out and ready while you do that. Maybe check the small barn out back and see if there's some wood that's not rotten. After we get a fire going, we'll get the truck unloaded and get to work."

Giving his brother a two-fingered mock salute, Jacob walked back out onto the porch and was pulling the door closed behind him when the plastic bag covering the window rattled. Pushing the door back open, he poked his head inside and whistled softly to get Fox's attention. When his brother looked at him, he dipped his head towards the window. "After I get some wood in here, I'll run back to the shop and see if we have a window to fit this pneumonia hole. If we don't have one, I'll run over to Kennery's and see if they have one or some windowpanes that fit. If nothing else, I'll pick up a sheet of plywood to cover it until we can order a new window." Without waiting for a reply, he closed the door and stepped off the porch, his gaze going to the plastic covered window once more as he made his way toward the back of the cabin.

Max was pulling her hair up into a high ponytail as she walked back into the living room, her eyes finding Fox squatting in front of the fireplace, his hands outstretched towards the roaring fire. Her breath caught in her throat as she studied the muscles rippling beneath his shirt when he picked up a log and tossed it onto the fire.

Hearing a gasp behind him, Fox turned his head and smiled up at Max. "Hope you don't mind that we built a fire. It was a bit chilly in here."

Averting her gaze, she shook her head. "It's perfectly fine." Her brow creased and she looked over at him again. "Did Jacob go back outside?"

Getting to his feet, Fox brushed the knees of his pants off as he shook his head. "He drove back into town to get something to fix that window over there."

"I was actually going to ask if you'd fix that today." Chewing her inner cheek, she looked towards the kitchen before glancing at Fox from the corner of her eye. "Are you hungry?"

"I could eat."

A smile spread across her face, and she gave him a curt nod as she walked towards the kitchen area. "Good, 'cause I'm starving, and it'd be awkward to eat in front of you. You like eggs and bacon? I..." Her words trailed off as she came to a sudden stop.

"What's wrong?" When she looked back at him, her mouth pulled down on one side, he took a step towards her. "Are you okay?"

Max held up a hand to stop him. "I'm fine, really. It's just... I was going to offer you bacon, but I don't think I can eat it after what happened last night."

Fox's back stiffened and he cocked his head to the side as he continued to study her face. "What exactly happened last night?"

"The piglets."

"The piglets? But I thought...?"

Max nodded. "They came back. There were about four or five of them on the porch again, playing and running around. I got a better look at them this time. They were so cute, Fox. I watched them until their momma stepped out of the darkness and led them back into the woods. I'm almost certain they aren't domesticated pigs."

His eyes widened and he looked in the direction of the porch before looking back at her. "You think you saw a wild sow and her litter? You didn't... you didn't go out there, did you?"

Shaking her head, she chuckled. "Absolutely not. I may be from the city, but I'm not an idiot. Besides, you should've seen the size of that momma pig." Holding her arms out, she attempted to show him how big the pig had been. "Massive."

His mouth twitched at the corner as he bit back a smile when she held her hand up to show him how tall the sow had been. "That's pretty big."

"I mean, maybe she was a little smaller but last night she looked like a giant to me." Sniffing, she walked into the kitchen and flicked on the light over the sink. "Pancakes okay?"

"More than okay. You need help or...?"

"I got it, thanks though." She looked over her shoulder when she heard the door open. "I'll come find you when it's ready."

Nodding, Fox stepped out the door. "I'm going to check the barn out back and see what all is in it. Maybe there's a windowpane we can use."

"There's a barn?" Turning, she leaned back against the counter as she dried her hands. "How am I just now finding this out?"

Pulling on his gloves, Fox shrugged. "You didn't look around when you moved in?"

Turning, she opened the nearest cabinet and lifted out a large glass measuring cup. "Haven't had time, if I'm being honest, and I don't recall it being in the real estate listing. I can't believe I didn't know about it. Where is it exactly?"

Sighing, Fox stepped back inside the cabin and closed the door before answering. "It's right out back. It's over to the... Tell you what, I can show you real quick."

Setting the bowl she had just taken from the cabinet down, she thought for a second and nodded. "Let me get a coat."

"If I remember correctly, there's a window that looks out over the backyard. You should be able to see it from there." When she hesitated, he waved a hand towards the back of the cabin. "Go into the back bedroom on the right and look out the window. The barn is set back a ways from the cabin, but you should be able to see it now that most of the leaves have fallen from the trees."

Stepping past him, she made her way down the hall and pushed open the door to the bedroom that she intended to set up as an office. Walking over to the window, she pushed the curtain aside and gasped before spinning and hurrying to the door. "Uh, Fox. Can you come in here?" She heard him chuckle and rolled her eyes. "Seriously, I..." Fox appeared at the other end of the hallway, his large frame blocking out the light from the front of the cabin.

"I was sure you'd be able to see the barn from that window. Maybe I'm mistaken and it's the other room." Stepping into the room, he noticed her pointing towards the window and he chuckled again before looking in the direction she was pointing. The smile fell from his face, and he took a giant step forward, pushing the curtains completely open as he stared out at the woods coated in a thick layer of snow. "Oh, this isn't good." Reaching down, he unclipped his phone and tapped the screen a few times before lifting the phone to his ear. When he didn't hear any ringing, he pulled the phone away and cursed softly when he saw the SOS in the upper right-hand side where the signal should be. "This is definitely not good."

Max spoke as she stared out in wonder at the snow-covered trees. "You didn't notice this when you were out on the porch a minute ago?"

Hurrying past her, his voice was gruff when he spoke. "I was busy answering your questions, remember?"

Heat flooded her cheeks as she stepped from the

room and followed him down the hall. "Maybe it's not as bad as it seems."

Opening the front door, Fox stepped out onto the porch and stared towards the driveway, now completely covered in several inches of snow. Releasing a heavy sigh, he walked over to the porch swing and lowered himself down to the cold wooden seat.

Max stood in the doorway and watched him as he sat there, his forearms propped on his thighs, his expression hard as stone as he stared out at the snow falling faster around them. "I don't understand. Isn't it too early for this kind of snow?" When the wind picked up and whipped snow towards her, she turned her head slightly and squinted at him as she waited for an answer.

His jaw muscles flexed as he shifted his gaze in her direction and spoke. "Early, yes, but not unheard of."

"Okay, so, it'll stop soon and ..." When she saw him shake his head, she lowered hers slightly. "It's not going to stop?"

"Oh, it'll stop, eventually. But this early and piling up this fast, a blizzard is brewing, and we are trapped up here with only a few groceries that you got the other day. Unless..." He looked up at her hopefully and arched a questioning brow.

"I..." She shrugged as embarrassment caused her

cheeks to flush hotly. "I didn't know I'd be needing to stock up. It's literally just me out here."

Getting to his feet, Fox began pacing the porch as he rubbed his forehead and spoke his thoughts aloud. "Okay. This isn't a big deal. I've been through worse. I can figure this out."

"We don't have to worry yet. Jacob should be back soon, right?" She stumbled back when Fox spun quickly to face her, his eyes narrowed into tiny slits.

"Did you pay attention to anything I just said? This is going to get really bad, real fast. The snow is already too deep for him to get up the road to the mountain, much less to the cabin. We're pretty much screwed, lady." When he noticed her mouth purse, he lowered his gaze and pinched the bridge of his nose. "Look, I'm sorry. I didn't mean to snap at you, it's just..."

"It's just you're stuck up here with me. I get it." Spinning on the ball of her foot, she walked back into the cabin and slammed the door behind her.

Fox stared at the door for a few minutes before knocking and turning the knob.

Max threw a glare over her shoulder when she heard the door softly close behind her. "You still want pancakes, or no?"

Running a hand through his hair, Fox shook his

head. "Thanks though." When he heard her muttering beneath her breath, he released a frustrated sigh of his own and walked over to stand in front of the picture window. He stared at the silk curtains before pushing them open and looking out at the snow as the storm quickly became a blizzard, the powerful winds lashing snow against the window. He could hear Max walking across the room, and he turned his head slightly in her direction when she stopped beside him, her arms crossed over her chest as she hugged herself tightly. "Look, I'm sorry for what I said out there. And you're wrong. I'm not upset that I'm stranded up here with you. I'm upset that I'm stranded at all." When he noticed the tears gathering at the corners of her eyes, he laid a hand on her shoulder and gave it a reassuring squeeze. "Hey, it's all right. We're going to be okay."

Sniffing back the tears that threatened to fall, she cut her eyes in his direction without turning her head. "I hope you're right."

Returning his attention to the window, he blindly reached out and clasped her fingers, squeezing them briefly before releasing her. "Me too, Max... me too."

Max felt a sense of unease settle over her as she walked back into the kitchen. The weight of the situation pressed down on her, making the cozy cabin feel suddenly claustrophobic. She started mixing the pancake batter, trying to focus on the task of cooking their breakfast to calm her nerves. The rhythmic stirring provided a small comfort, but her mind kept wandering back to the snowstorm raging outside.

As she poured the batter onto the hot griddle, the sizzle of the batter meeting the heat filled the silence. She found herself glancing towards the window more often than necessary, her thoughts drifting to Jacob. What if he couldn't make it back? What if he was stuck somewhere in the snow?

Fox's voice broke through her thoughts. "Pancakes smell good."

She turned to find him leaning against the kitchen doorway, his expression softer than before. "Thanks. I cooked you some, even though you said you didn't want any. They should be ready in a few minutes."

He nodded and stepped closer, the tension between them easing slightly. "I really am sorry about earlier. I didn't mean to snap. This whole situation just... caught me off guard."

Max offered a small smile. "It's okay. I'm not exactly handling it well myself." She looked up at the ceiling when she heard several thuds against the roof as the wind howled outside. "I hope I don't lose anymore shingles."

"It was probably just pinecones falling from the wind. I'll check it out later when I can get up there." Fox walked across the room and pulled open the cabinet where he knew the plates were kept. Pulling two down, he gathered up the utensils and carried them over to the table. He looked up in time to catch Max glancing over her shoulder, a soft smile curving the corners of her mouth. "I'll get a pot of coffee started, if you want."

"That would be great, thanks." She pointed towards the pantry with her spatula before turning back to the stove. "Coffee and filters are in there, along with the bottled water."

Nodding, he walked over to the pantry, pulled the door open, and squinted into the darkness. "You'll want to install a light in here before summer. I'd suggest an automatic one that comes on as soon as you open the door or..."

"There's already a light in there. The switch is to your left." Max looked over when she heard him flicking the switch repeatedly. Sighing, she shook her head. "Light must be blown, and I don't have anymore. Let me get you a flashlight."

"It's fine. I'll just use the light on my phone for now." Shining the light towards the shelves, he scanned the contents until he found what he was after.

As they sat down to eat, Max stared at the fire and took a deep breath through her nose before slowly releasing it and asking the question she feared the answer to. "Do we have enough wood to last a while?"

Lowering his fork, Fox lifted his coffee cup and took a drink before answering. "I honestly don't think we do. I still need to check the barn, so there may be some in there. If not, I'll go out and gather more if it comes to that."

Max shifted her eyes towards the man sitting opposite her. "If you need to gather wood, I'll help you." When he opened his mouth, no doubt to protest, she shook her head. "I'll help."

Nodding slightly, Fox picked up his fork and resumed eating, a small smile tugging at the corner of his mouth.

· · ·

After breakfast, they worked together, side by side, to clean up the kitchen. Max washing and Fox drying. She tried to ignore the sensations she felt every time his hand brushed against hers when she passed him a dish. Looking at him from the corner of her eye, she watched him as he carefully dried the plate she had handed him before gently placing it back inside the cabinet.

Once the kitchen was clean, Fox suggested they check the supplies and see what they had to work with. Using a flashlight, they rummaged through the pantry before moving on to the cabinets, taking inventory of the food and essentials. The supply was meager but manageable if they were careful.

"We'll have to ration what you have." Glancing at Max, Fox finished speaking, his words a soft whisper. "And maybe come up with a plan if the snow doesn't let up soon."

Max nodded, feeling a sense of determination rise within her. "We'll figure it out. We have to."

Fox's phone buzzed, drawing their attention. "Looks like I have signal again. With any luck, Jacob can get up here and we can get down the mountain to get you some supplies." He checked the message and let out a relieved breath, before his shoulders sagged. "It's Jacob. The good news, he's stuck in town and he's okay.

The bad news, he says the roads are almost impassable, but he's safe and will come back as soon as he can."

A mixture of relief and despair washed over her, and she forced herself to smile. "That's good to hear. I'm so glad your brother is safe." Drawing a deep breath through her nose, she released it as she got to her feet. "I think I'll get the guest room set up for you, so you don't have to bunk out on the couch."

Standing, Fox reached for his coat as he spoke. "I'll go check out the barn while you do that. Hopefully I can find something to go over that window. How much would you mind if I have to board it up?"

Max looked towards the plastic covered window and shook her head. "I don't mind a bit. Do what needs to be done to keep the heat inside."

Giving her a mock salute with two fingers, Fox spoke as he turned towards the door. "Yes ma'am. I'll be back shortly."

Max waited for him to walk out and close the door behind himself before releasing another sigh as she turned to walk down the short hallway.

They spent the rest of the day working around the cabin, doing what they could to prepare for the days ahead. Fox boarded up the window, and Max focused on organizing and making the cabin as comfortable as possible. As evening fell, they settled by the fire, the warmth and crackling of the flames providing a soothing backdrop to their conversation.

Fox shared stories about his childhood, his hiking adventures, and his passion for photography, and Max found herself opening up about her life in the city, her career, and what her plans were for the cabin once she got settled in. The more they talked, the more they realized they had in common, and the initial tension between them began to dissipate.

As the fire burned low and the cabin grew quiet, Max felt a sense of peace settle over her. Despite the storm outside and the uncertainty of what lay ahead, she felt a connection with Fox that she hadn't expected. When her eyes grew heavy, she bid Fox goodnight and made her way towards her bedroom. Stopping at the door, she looked back towards the living room where Fox was banking the fire for the night, and she bit down on her bottom lip. They had known each other for less than a week and the thought of him sleeping in the room next to hers was both frightening and comforting. Walking into her room, she pushed her door closed and, after hesitating a few seconds, turned the lock on the handle before undressing and crawling beneath her blankets.

She held her breath when she heard the door next to her room close, and she released it when the guest bed creaked. Rolling to her side, she pulled the blankets up to her chin and closed her eyes. She drifted off to sleep with a smile on her face, dreaming of a future where the cabin was restored, and she had found her place in this new, wild world.

ninE

Holding his hand out, Fox motioned with his fingers. "Hand me a half-inch socket and ratchet, would ya?"

Handing him the tools, Max squinted at the round piece of metal Fox was bolting into the wall. "Are you sure that's right? I don't know how good that'll hold up once I have all of my clothes hung on the rod."

Casting a quick glance over his shoulder, Fox nodded. "Trust me, it'll hold." Feigning a cough, he cleared his throat and spoke, his voice deep and raspy. "Can I bother you for a bottle of water, please?"

Max hesitated a second before stepping back. "Yeah, sure. I'll be right back."

When he was sure she was out of the room, Fox dropped his head and closed his eyes. "This is going to be a long damn day, I just know it." He jerked in surprise and raised his head up when the phone on his hip chirped, signaling a text message. Tightening down the last bolt, he stepped from the closet and pulled his phone from its holster.

JACOB:

> They've got the roads in town cleared, but it'll be a bit before I can get back up there. Joseph called and he needs me to come over and take a look at his furnace. Be back ASAP.

Looking towards the window, Fox shook his head and quickly tapped out a response.

FOX:

> It's still snowing up this way. Looked like another storm front is moving in when I went out earlier. Wait for my all clear before attempting to make the drive up that switchback.

He stared at his phone and waited for a reply. When he didn't get one, he released a deep sigh and returned his phone to the holster before turning and walking towards the door in search of Max and his bottle of water. Stepping from the room, he pulled up short when he saw Max standing in the middle of the hallway, her head turned towards the bathroom, a bottle of water clutched to her chest. "Everything all right?"

Max shook her head without looking at him. "I think we've sprung another leak."

"Tell me you're joking?"

Cutting her eyes in his direction, she arched an eyebrow and dipped her head towards the doorway. "Come listen for yourself. I hear running water."

Rubbing the spot between his eyes, he walked over to stand beside her and held her gaze as he listened. After a few minutes, he shook his head. "That's not a leak."

"It's clearly running water, Fox. If it's not a leak, what the hell is it?"

Fox shrugged, his mouth pulling down at the corners. "Don't know yet. Does this place have a basement?"

It was Max's turn to shrug. "Your guess is as good as mine." Remembering the bottle of water, she held it out and waited for him to take it. "You know, now that I think about it, there is a door inside the pantry. I meant to check it out the other day, but never got around to it."

Lowering the bottle, Fox capped it and wiped his mouth with the back of his hand. "Show me."

Crooking her fingers, she motioned for him to follow her as she turned and moved back toward the front of the cabin.

Opening the pantry door, Max was feeling for the light switch when she remembered the blown bulb. She was turning towards Fox when light filled the small room, illuminating the shelves lined sparingly with canned goods. "Thanks."

"No problem." Fox passed her the flashlight before pulling his cellphone from his pocket and tapping on the flashlight icon.

Stepping fully into the pantry, Max pushed aside a hanging apron and a mop to reveal the door she had seen when she was setting up the pantry. "Here." She looked back at him as she ran her hand over the old wooden door. "I think this might lead to the basement."

Fox reached past her and tried the handle. It was stiff, but after a moment of jiggling it, the door creaked open, revealing a dark, narrow staircase leading down.

A cold draft wafted up, carrying the musty scent of earth and damp wood.

Max shivered. "Why does there always have to be a creepy basement?"

Fox smirked, stepping past her to descend the stairs. "Stay here. I'll check it out."

"Like hell I will." Clutching the flashlight with both hands, she shined it towards the stairs and followed him down.

The staircase groaned under their weight, and with each step, the sound of running water grew louder. At the bottom, they found themselves in a low-ceilinged, dirt-floored space. It was dimly lit by a small window high up on one wall, half-covered by snow from outside.

Max swung the flashlight around the room, the beam landing on old wooden furniture and stacks of forgotten boxes. In the corner, the source of the sound became clear: a steady stream of water was trickling down the wall beneath a boarded-up window, pooling on the floor.

"Great." Max shook her head in frustration. "Just what we needed. Something else to fix."

Fox examined the gap between the wall and the board, his brow furrowed. "We'll need to seal this up, but we can't do much more until I can get to town to get the right supplies. We'll have to make do for now." He looked around the basement, spotting an old bucket and some rags. "We can at least try to control the water flow as much as possible. We can use those old rags to stuff in the gaps and it should help a bit."

Max nodded, setting the flashlight down to help him. "Okay, let's do it."

Together, they worked in silence, creating a makeshift barrier with the rags and positioning the bucket to catch as much of the water as possible. It wasn't a perfect solution, but it was better than letting the water continue to spread unchecked.

After a while, Fox stepped back, wiping his hands on his jeans. "That should hold for now. We'll need to keep an eye on it, though."

Max sighed heavily as she picked up the flashlight and shined the beam at the walls around the basement. "Doesn't appear to be any water coming from anywhere else." Looking back at Fox, she dipped her head in a slight nod. "Thanks for helping. I know this isn't what you had in mind when I hired you."

He gave her a small smile. "It's not a problem. Let's head back up. It's freezing down here."

Back in the warmth of the living room, they both took a moment to warm their hands by the fire. Max glanced at Fox from the corner of her eye, feeling a strange mix of gratitude and frustration. "What are we going to do if the snow keeps up like this?"

Fox shrugged, taking a sip from his water bottle. "We'll manage. We've got a fire, some food, and enough work to keep ourselves busy. We'll be okay."

Max remained silent as she thought about what he'd just said. Despite the challenges, she felt a growing sense of determination. They would get through this, one way or another.

Later, as evening began to fall, Max busied herself in the kitchen, preparing a simple dinner. The cabin was cozy, the fire casting a warm glow across the room, and the scent of cooking filled the air. Fox had taken a seat at the table, looking through his phone and occasionally glancing out the window at the snow that showed no sign of letting up.

"It's not much but it's hot." Max gave him a tight-lipped smile as she placed a pot of stew on the table. "I hope you like vegetable stew."

Fox looked up, smiling. "Sounds perfect. Thanks, Max."

They sat down to eat, the warmth of the stew and the fire creating a comforting atmosphere despite the howling wind outside. They talked about their plans for the next day and the work that still needed to be done on the cabin.

As they finished dinner, Max stood up to clear the table. Fox reached out, touching her arm gently. "You don't have to do it all yourself. Let me help."

She smiled, appreciating the offer. "Thanks. I'll get the dishes, and you can wipe down the table and put away the leftovers."

They worked together to clean up the kitchen, Max washing the dishes while Fox wiped down the table and cookstove before putting away the leftover stew and cornbread. Max found herself feeling more at ease, the earlier tension fading away. She was thankful for Fox's company, but she knew he must be ready to get back home.

After the kitchen was clean, they settled in front of the fire again. Max brought out a deck of cards, and they played a few hands of poker, laughing and talking as the evening wore on. It felt good to relax, to forget about the snow steadily piling up outside for a while, and to enjoy each other's company.

As the night grew late, Fox stoked the fire, adding another log to keep it burning through the night. "We should get some rest." Maneuvering the fireplace gate around, he made sure it was in place before straightening to his full height, adjusting the damper, and turning to face her. "That should keep the fire going until morning. Hopefully, this storm will blow over by the time we wake up and I can get you more wood. What we have isn't going to last much longer."

Max nodded, stifling a yawn, as she got to her feet. "Goodnight, Fox."

"Goodnight, Max." His gaze lingered on her for a moment before he turned and walked down the hall towards the spare room where he had been sleeping. He stopped and looked back over his shoulder when Max called out his name. "Yeah?"

"If you want, I have a package of men's boxers you can have." When he arched an eyebrow at her, she rolled her eyes and shook her head. "They're mine. I like wearing them when I'm slouching around the house. I buy them in a larger size, so they might fit you. In the morning, if it's still snowing, you can use the washer and dryer to wash your clothes."

Dimples appeared at the corners of his mouth when he gave her a teasing smile. "You think I stink or something?"

Max snorted and rolled her eyes again. "Not yet, but let's stop it before it happens, yeah?"

Fox was silent for a few seconds before dipping his head in a nod. "All right. In that case, I'll get a shower before I call it a night then."

Max headed to her own room to get the package of

boxers and tried to stave off the image of a naked Fox in her shower.

After giving him the boxers, she went back into her room and closed the door. Changing into her pajama's, she tried to ignore the sounds coming from the bathroom as Fox prepared to take his shower. She wasn't a prude and could admit to herself that she found Fox attractive and would often wonder what his mouth would feel like pressed against hers.

As she settled into bed, she thought about the days ahead, the work that still needed to be done, and the unexpected feelings she was developing for Fox. She closed her eyes against the desire burning low in her stomach and pulled a pillow over her head in an attempt to drown out the sound of him humming as he showered.

"Max?"

Mumbling, Max rolled to her side and swatted at the hand pushing against her shoulder. "Go away."

"Max, come on, wake up."

Opening her eyes, she stared at the knees of Fox's black jeans. "I'm awake. What do you want?"

"I have to go out for wood."

Rolling to her back, she flung an arm over her eyes as she pulled the blanket up over her chest. "Why do I need to know this, Fox?" She heard him snort before he spoke.

"Because you're going with me, remember?"

Lifting her arm, she turned her head and looked up at him. "I beg your pardon?"

Snapping his fingers, he motioned for her to sit up.

"You said you'd help gather firewood. Besides, you've got to learn how to find dry wood when the ground is covered in snow and I'm going to teach you."

Her eyes widened before she leveled a glare at him. "Did... did you just snap your fingers at me?"

Leaning forward, he grasped the edge of the blanket and pulled it from the bed, carrying it with him as he walked from the room. "I'll be waiting in the kitchen. Hurry up though, it's starting to snow again."

Glaring at the empty doorway, Max made a rude gesture before kicking the top sheet off and sitting up with a huff of annoyance. Raising her voice, she yelled out to him as she got to her feet. "I don't like you very much right now. I want you to know that. You're bossy and arrogant." She squeaked when his head appeared around the edge of the door.

"You'll get used to it." Fox smiled at her and winked before pulling his head back when she threw a pillow in his direction. Her angry growl caused him to laugh softly as he walked down the hallway towards the front of the cabin.

Max continued to grumble as she pulled a pair of sweatpants on over her jeans and jerked the hem of her sweatshirt down as she looked around for her hiking boots. "*You'll get used to it*. Get used to it my butt. I should make him stay in the barn. See how bossy he is after a night out there." She straightened and spun to look at the door when she heard him clear his throat. "How long have you been standing there?"

Remaining silent, Fox held out a mug of steaming coffee and walked away once she took it.

"Thank you!" When he didn't respond, she sniffed the coffee before taking a sip, sighing in bliss as the hot liquid warmed her from the inside out. Sitting on the foot of the bed, she felt her anger slowly melt away and instantly regretted her earlier words. Looking towards the doorway, she released a deep breath and picked up her boots before standing and walking from the room. Fox turned from the window when she entered the front room, and she lifted the cup in greeting. "Thank you for this. I'm... I'm sorry about earlier. I didn't mean it."

"Didn't mean it or didn't mean for me to hear it?"

Lowering her gaze in embarrassment, she walked to the couch and sat down. "Both. I just, I'm not accustomed to being cooped up, much less with someone that's so..." She waved her hand in his direction and arched a brow when he grunted before turning to face the window again, his hands clasped behind his back. "What's that supposed to mean?"

Fox shrugged dismissively. "Nothing."

"Something, obviously."

Looking over his shoulder, he shrugged again. "I'm not going to argue with you."

"I'm not trying to argue."

"Aren't you though?"

Her mouth dropped open as she stared up at him. "I'm trying to apologize, but you won't let me."

Giving her a curt nod, he faced the window again. "Apology accepted."

"But I..." When he looked back over his shoulder, she snapped her mouth closed and shook her head before returning her attention to her boots. "I need to eat something before we get started."

"There's biscuits and gravy on the stove."

Max's hands stilled and she raised her head enough to look up at his back. "You cooked?"

Turning, he leaned back against the windowsill and crossed his arms over his chest as he returned her gaze. "Is that a problem?"

Max shook her head slowly before tying her boot and getting to her feet. "Not at all. Have you eaten then?"

It was Fox's turn to shake his head. "I was waiting for you." Pushing away from the windowsill, he strode into the kitchen and pulled two plates from the cabinet, turning as Max entered behind him and handing her a plate. "If we eat quickly, we might be able to get enough wood gathered to last a few days before the snow gets bad again."

"You don't think it's over?"

Fox shook his head as he broke apart a biscuit and laid it on his plate before scooping out a ladle full of gravy and pouring it over the top of the biscuit. "I heard thunder in the distance earlier." Stepping to the side, he offered her the ladle.

Taking the ladle, she scooped gravy onto her plate before reaching for a biscuit. "Could it be a thunderstorm?"

Carrying his plate to the table, Fox pulled out a chair and sat down, waiting for her to sit before replying. "Not necessarily. It's been known to thunder during a blizzard."

Max groaned as she tore her biscuit into pieces. "I wish it would stop long enough for us to find a way off this mountain. We can't live forever on biscuits and gravy and what few canned goods we have left. I mean... we probably could but I wouldn't want to."

Fox nodded in agreement as he chewed his food.

Swallowing, he forked up another bite as he spoke. "Well, hopefully, Jacob will think to find a snowmobile and come up to check on us. If he does, I can go into town and get supplies for you."

Max's fork stopped midway to her mouth. "For me? You mean... you're saying you'd leave me up here alone? Trapped by mountains of snow?"

Fox stared at her as he slowly chewed the bite he had just taken. Swallowing, he took a drink of coffee and cleared his throat before speaking. "Max, you know I can't stay up here with you, right? I have to go home eventually."

"I know. It's just..." Her nose twitched as she looked towards the window. "I didn't think it would be like this when I bought the place. I pictured tranquil nights and the silence of the woods. It never dawned on me that winters would be so ... isolating. I can handle being alone when I know I can leave at any point."

"You just don't know if you can handle being alone when you can't leave. I get it, I do. I love these mountains, but being trapped up here is not my idea of a good time." When she remained silent, he picked up his fork again and continued eating.

Max forced herself not to cry as she finished her breakfast. She knew she couldn't beg him not to leave, but she'd be lying to herself if she said the thought hadn't crossed her mind while he had been talking.

Fox stared down at Max and clutched his stomach as he tried to stop laughing.

"It's not funny!"

"It... it kinda... is." Reaching up, he wiped beneath his eyes with the back of his gloved hand.

Crossing her arms over the top of her snow-covered chest, Max mentally tapped her foot as she waited for him to get control of his laughter. When he took a deep breath and released it, she arched a brow and sucked her teeth before speaking. "You going to stand there laughing all day or you going to help me out of this drift?"

Dropping to one knee, Fox took hold of her hands and pulled as he tried to stand up before quickly dropping back to his knee. "Wow, you really are stuck in there."

"Still funny?"

His mouth twitched as he leaned forward and

motioned for her to lift her arms so he could wrap his arms around her.

Max shuddered and tried to ignore the feel of his hot breath against her ear as he grunted with the effort to pull her from the snow. "Fox?" Her voice sounded breathy to her own ears, and she blushed when he spoke again.

"Yeah, Max?"

"Let me... Maybe stand up and pull up on my arms while I try to move my feet enough to make room for me to step up and, I don't know, climb out of the snow like walking up steps." She released the breath she had been holding when he moved back and got to his feet.

Grasping her by the wrists, Fox pulled up, his teeth clenched as he tried lifting her from the drift she had stepped in. "Let's try rocking you back and forth to make the hole bigger around your waist."

"Okay." Tugging her hands free, she rocked back and forth and side to side until she could twist her hips. Smiling, she looked up at him. "I think it worked." Raising her hands, she motioned for him to take them again and continued to twist herself as he pulled up.

As she slowly began to break free of the snow, Fox took small steps backward until her legs were visible.

"Hold still." Keeping pressure on her so she didn't slide back down, he worked his way down her body until he could wrap his arms around her waist. "Ready?"

"Yes." Holding onto his shoulders, she clutched at him as he stood to his full height, finally pulling her free of the snowdrift. Her grip loosened and she waited for him to set her back on her feet now that she was free. Instead, he began walking backward, his cheek planted firmly against her chest. "Ummm... Fox?"

His voice was deep and raspy when he spoke. "I want to make sure you're nowhere near that drift before I put you down."

"Oh... okay then." Her heart thumped against her ribcage so hard, she was sure he could feel it against his cheek. When she felt her feet touch the ground, she quickly stepped back but reached out to clutch his arm when her right foot slipped.

Grabbing her wrist, Fox held her to keep her from falling. "Take a minute to get your footing."

A humorless laugh escaped Max's lips before she could stop it. "Trust me, I'm trying. The ground slopes down here a bit."

"Okay. I'm going to take a step back and you try to walk with me." When she nodded, he slid one foot back and then the other until she was able to stand without slipping. "Got it?"

Releasing his arm, she slowly lifted her hands and nodded. "Thanks." Looking over her shoulder, she shuddered and took a tentative step towards Fox. "With the ground sloping like that, I wonder now if there isn't a hole or something where I stepped."

"Could be. Maybe you should follow behind me from now on." He expected her to argue, but she surprised him by nodding in agreement.

"Wanna know something about me that no one else knows?" When he remained silent, she continued speaking. "I have a fear of the ground collapsing beneath me. Reading about sinkholes absolutely terrifies me."

Fox dropped his head in his hands and groaned. "I'm such a jerk for laughing." Raising his head, he stared down at her. "I am so sorry, Max. I had no idea you were scared."

Shrugging, she took another step forward. "I was scared but I could feel the ground or something solid beneath my feet." Looking up at the darkening sky, she shivered and pointed at the wood he had sat down when she fell. "We should get this home before it gets dark."

Fox watched her pick up a few of the logs, his brow creasing in concern when he noticed a rip in her sweatpants and a red patch growing on the back of her left leg. "Max, are you hurt?"

Straightening with her arms filled with wood, she blew her bangs from her face and turned to face him. "No, why?" Her eyes widened when he stepped towards her and dropped to a knee. Her instinct was to step away, but he quickly clutched at her leg to stop her.

"Stand still."

"What are you d...?" She gasped and released a small cry of pain when he touched her thigh. The wood fell back to the ground, and she had to clutch at Fox's shoulders to keep from falling.

Gently parting the sweatpants material, he saw that her jeans were also ripped, and a deep cut ran the length of the rip. Working quickly, he pulled his scarf from around his neck and tied it tightly around her leg to cover the cut before getting to his feet. "We have to get you off this mountain."

"How bad is it? I didn't even feel anything until you touched it."

"It's deep enough that you could use some stitches. I'm guessing the cold numbed your legs before you fell and also slowed the bleeding." Bending, he scooped her up into his arms and started walking.

Looking back over his shoulder at the wood, she

began struggling to get down. "What are you doing? We need that wood, Fox."

"Be still. I can get you down the mountain and back to the cabin faster if I carry you." When she grew still, he held her closer and picked up his pace, his breath coming in panting gasps as his eyes scanned the woods, hoping they didn't cross paths with a hungry grizzly or mountain lion.

When they reached the cabin, Fox stepped up onto the porch before lowering Max back to her feet. Trying the doorknob, he found the door locked and looked down at Max. "Key?"

Unzipping a pocket on her coat, she pulled her keys out and passed them to him. When the door opened, she stepped past him and limped inside, wincing with each step, and went to lay on the sofa with a huff, her face pale with pain.

Fox stared at her, his expression tight with concern as he knelt beside her. "I need to take your pants off."

Max released a humorless laugh. "Not exactly the situation I pictured when..." Her words ended abruptly, and she squeezed her eyes closed as embarrassment engulfed her. "Never mind. There's a first aid kit in the bathroom. It should be under the sink or maybe in the linen closet."

"I'll be right back."

When Fox disappeared down the hallway, Max struggled to sit up before standing and hurrying out of her sweatpants and jeans. Looking back at her leg, she turned in a slow circle as she used the leg of her sweatpants to wipe away most of the blood, sucking a hissing breath through her teeth as pain flared to life with each swipe of the material. Hearing the cupboard door slam shut, she quickly lowered herself back onto the couch, before stretching out onto her stomach.

Entering the room again with the supplies from the bathroom, he noted she had taken off her pants and averted his gaze as he returned to her side. His breath caught in his throat when he got his first clear view of the wound on the back of her thigh.

Max stared up at him from beneath drooping eyelids. "I tried to wipe some of the blood away. Hurts like hell."

His brow furrowed as he assessed the wound. "You need stitches." He looked up when she drew a hissing breath through her teeth.

Max winced slightly but managed a weak smile. "I've had worse."

"Doesn't mean we shouldn't take care of this properly." Fox's voice was gentle, his hands steady as he wiped at the blood trickling from the wound.

"Are you... good at stitching?" Max's voice betrayed her nervousness, though she tried to keep her tone light.

Fox chuckled softly, a hint of amusement coloring his worry. "I've had my share of practice. But ideally, we'd get you to a doctor."

Max glanced around the cabin, her gaze settling on the window through which the snow continued to fall heavily. "Doesn't look like that's happening anytime soon."

"No." His voice had a grim undertone to it when he continued. "We're stuck here until the storm lets up."

Sighing softly, Max closed her eyes briefly, gathering her courage around her like a blanket. "All right, then. Do what you have to do."

Fox nodded and carefully lifted away the gauze pad he had been using to staunch the blood. He examined the wound again, his expression thoughtful. "It's not bleeding heavily now, which is good. But we need to clean it properly before I stitch it up."

Max cried out and bit down on the side of her wrist. Fox closed his hand over her naked calf when she flinched beneath his touch. "I know it hurts, but you need to try to be still. I have to get it cleaned out as much as I can before I pinch it closed." Picking up a bottle of alcohol, he stared at the back of her head as he tightened his hold on her leg. "This is going to sting a little."

Hot tears of pain coursed down her cheeks, and she sniffed as she nodded, her fingers gripping the edge of the sofa as she braced herself for the sting. She felt the coldness of the liquid seconds before the burn set in. A scream tore its way from her throat, and she buried her face in the throw pillow to try to smother it. Dizziness washed over her, and she let the darkness take her as she lost consciousness.

Fox breathed a sigh of relief when her body grew limp beneath his hold. Reaching forward, he gently moved her head, so her face wasn't pressed into the pillow obstructing her breathing. Returning his attention to her thigh, he studied the cut again before picking up the bottle of peroxide and flipping the cap open. Working quickly, he finished cleaning up the cut before pinching the edges together and picking up the threaded needle he had found in her medical kit. Gritting his teeth, he pushed the needle through her skin and lifted his eyes to watch her face for signs of her regaining consciousness as he pulled the thread tight.

Max's eyelids fluttered, and a groan escaped her lips. "Just a few more stitches." Fox spoke softly, his voice steady despite the tension in the room. He worked swiftly and methodically, his stitches neat and precise. Once he finished, he applied a fresh dressing and secured it in place. "There. All done." Giving her a smile, he gathered up the soiled gauze and carried it into the kitchen to the trash before going to the sink and washing his hands. Returning to the living room, he pulled a throw blanket from the back of the couch and settled it over Max before picking up the rest of the supplies. He was turning to take them back to the bathroom when Max said his name softly. Looking back at her, he moved to help her sit when she shook her head and waved him off.

Shifting so that most of her weight was on her right side, Max let out a shaky breath as she adjusted her position on the couch, feeling a wave of relief wash over her when the stinging pain she expected was only a dull ache. "Thank you, Fox."

He nodded, his expression softening as he met her heavy-lidded gaze. "You're welcome, Max." Walking from the room, Fox entered the bathroom and put away the supplies before resting his hands on the edge of the sink and lowering his head, his eyes squeezed shut as he drew deep steadying breaths through his nose and released them slowly. He didn't exactly lie to Max when he told her he had a little experience with stitches, but he had never sewn up someone other than himself. After several minutes, he flushed the toilet and washed his hands before returning to Max's side.

They sat in silence for a moment, the only sound the crackling of the fire and the distant howl of the wind outside. Max glanced at Fox, grateful for his presence and his steady hands that had just stitched her back together.

"You know..." She waited for him to look down at her before continuing. "Despite everything, I'm glad you're here with me."

Fox looked at her, his gaze warm with understanding. "Me too, Max."

A small smile tugged at Max's lips. "I suppose being stuck in a blizzard isn't all bad when you have good company."

Fox chuckled softly. "Guess not."

As they settled into a comfortable quiet again, the tension of the day began to melt away. Max shifted on the sofa until she was lying on her side, her back facing the window. Staring into the fire, she could feel exhaustion seeping into her bones. She glanced at Fox, noticing the lines of fatigue and concern that etched his face.

"You should rest too." Her voice was soft when she spoke, and she wondered briefly if he had heard her.

Fox hesitated for a moment before nodding. "Yeah, I guess I could use some sleep."

Sitting up slightly, Max patted the empty space where her head had been lying on the sofa. "Come on, then. We can keep each other company."

With a grateful smile, Fox sat down and held his arm up until she lay her head in his lap. After an awkward moment, he rested his hand on her shoulder and leaned his head back against the sofa, closing his eyes as they both found a semblance of comfort in each other's presence. The fire crackled on, casting flickering shadows on the walls of the cabin as the storm gained strength and tree branches lashed against the sides of the cabin.

At that moment, as they faced the uncertainty of the storm and the isolation of the mountain, Max found herself grateful for the unexpected bond that had formed between them. As she drifted off to sleep, she couldn't help but smile when she felt Fox twirling a strand of her hair around his finger.

eleven

Stepping from the cabin, Fox breathed in the cold mountain air, the icy wind cutting through his jacket and stinging his skin. He released it with a tired sigh as he walked over to the porch swing and sat down. The wood creaked under his weight, a familiar, comforting sound in the otherwise silent landscape. Leaning his head back, he closed his eyes for a few minutes, savoring the stillness, before pulling his phone from the case on his side and lifting it to look at the screen for what felt like the millionth time. His eyes grew wide, and his head shot up when he saw a single bar in the upper right-hand corner.

With a surge of hope, he tapped the phone icon, selected Jacob's name, and touched the call icon with his thumb. Holding the phone to his ear, his eyes closed when he heard a ring, and he rubbed a hand over his face as he waited for Jacob to answer. Each second felt like an eternity.

"Fox?"

Fox's brow creased and he pulled the phone away to look at the name of the person he had called before putting it back to his ear and speaking. "Kendall? Why are you answering Jacob's phone?"

A watery sob came over the line before the woman responded. *"He's hurt bad, Fox."*

Fox sprang to his feet and stepped off the side of the porch, his boots crunching in the snow. "What do you mean he's hurt? What happened?"

"Six days ago, he told me he needed to go fix a furnace for Mr. Wallace and then he was going try to make it up to Mirror Springs Mountain to get you. They don't really know what happened, but he lost control of the truck and rolled it down the side of Pine Gulch."

"Pine Gulch? What was he doing over there? He should've been back..."

Kendall cut him off before he could finish his sentence. *"I keep asking myself the same thing, Fox. We can only guess at this point. Like I said, we don't really know what happened. The sheriff thinks he got turned around in the blizzard and either hit a patch of black ice or maybe he swerved to avoid an oncoming vehicle.*

Whatever the case, he was down there for several hours before someone found him. Though how they even saw him is beyond me."

She grew quiet for a second, and Fox felt his stomach tighten and his legs grow weak when she spoke again.

"We can't get him to wake up, Fox."

Reaching out blindly, he wrapped his arm around the nearest tree and used it to hold himself up. "You said he's hurt bad. Just how bad is it, Kendall?"

She sniffed before answering. *"His legs are busted up, he has a broken arm, a few broken ribs, and... and head trauma. He... he was ejected from the truck, and they found him lying at the base of a tree. The doctor said the storm may have caused the accident, but the cold temperatures most likely saved his life."*

Tears pricked the back of his eyes, and he had to take several deep breaths to keep them under control so he could speak. "I'm on my way." When there was no reply, his hand tightened on the phone, and he raised his voice and spoke again. "Do you hear me, Kendall? I'm on my way."

Fox barely heard her when she finally answered, and he turned his head slightly, hoping the signal wouldn't fade out. *"Fox, stay there. I don't know how bad it is up there, but here, it is piled up several feet and getting worse. They're calling for another blizzard tonight. There's no way you can make it off that mountain before it hits."*

Anger coiled in Fox's stomach, and his fingers bit into the bark of the tree. "I can't just sit up on this mountain and do nothing, damn it!"

Kendall's voice was soft when she spoke. *"He's going to need you more than ever when he wakes up, Fox. You can't risk getting caught up in the blizzard like he did. Just sit it out, please. Don't let Jacob wake up to the news that his big brother froze to death trying to make it down the mountain."*

His breath caught in his throat, and he spoke in a gruff voice. "And if he dies, I have to live with the knowledge that he died trying to save me."

"Don't talk like that! He's going to wake up, Fox. This isn't your fault. You have to believe that."

"How can I believe that when you said yourself, he was on his way here when he wrecked?" His hand shook as he cursed and pulled the phone away from his ear when the phone beeped, indicating he had lost signal. He longed to throw the phone deep into the wilderness, to forget he ever called Jacob's number. Instead, he returned the phone to the case on his hip before sinking to his knees in the snow and burying his face in his hands as he let the tears flow freely.

The cold bit into his skin, the reality of it grounding him even as the weight of his grief threatened to pull him under. The wind howled through the trees, and he shivered, his breath coming in ragged sobs that misted in the frigid air. He stayed there, feeling the snow seep through his pants and the frost nip at his fingers, the harshness of the mountain a stark contrast to the warmth of his tears.

Minutes passed, or maybe hours, time seemed to stretch endlessly. The cold was becoming unbearable, and Fox knew he needed to move, needed to get back inside before he caught pneumonia or worse. He forced himself to stand, his legs stiff and unsteady. He stumbled back to the cabin; his body numb but his mind racing. Inside, the warmth from the fire was a welcome relief from the bitter cold outside. The crackling flames promised warmth and comfort, but it did little to thaw the fear and anxiety that had settled deep in his bones.

He moved on autopilot, gathering supplies he might need for the journey down the mountain. Walking into the room he had been using, he grabbed up the sweatpants Max had given him to wear while his clothes washed and carried them out to the living room where his tool bag was. Removing all the tools except his flashlight, he lay the sweatpants on the back of a chair before going into the bathroom to get the first aid kit. Moving to the pantry, he grabbed up a box of crackers and several cans of beans and carried the to the tool bag. As he packed, his mind raced with memories of Jacob—the way his brother's laughter could fill a room, the times they'd spent together exploring these very mountains. The thought of Jacob lying injured and unconscious in some sterile hospital room, made Fox's chest tighten.

His phone buzzed, startling him and he quickly pulled it from the clip, hoping against hope for good news, but it was just a weather alert. Another blizzard was indeed on the way. He cursed under his breath and threw the phone onto the table.

Just then, Max hobbled into the kitchen and stopped in her tracks when she saw him standing at the kitchen table. She took one look at Fox and knew something was wrong. "Fox, what's going on? You look like you've seen a ghost."

Lifting his head, Fox looked at her, his face pale and strained. "It's Jacob. He's been in an accident. He's in the hospital, and... he's in bad shape."

Max's eyes widened in shock. "What happened?"

Fox explained everything, his voice trembling as he recounted Kendall's call. Max listened, her expression shifting from shock to concern. When he finished, she stepped closer and put a hand on his arm. "Fox, I'm so sorry. But you know you can't go down the mountain tonight. The blizzard is coming, and it's too dangerous."

"I know." His voice broke and he cleared his throat before continuing. "But I can't just stay here. I need to be with him. I need to know he's okay."

Max squeezed his arm. "And you will be with him, but not tonight. You need to wait until it's safe. If you go out there now, you could get hurt and no one will be able to help you. Think about what Jacob would want. He wouldn't want you risking your life."

Fox ran a hand through his hair, frustration and helplessness warring within him. "It's just so hard, Max. Knowing he's lying there, hurt and possibly dying. I feel like I'm failing him by not being there."

"You're not failing him." Max gave his arm a firm squeeze until he looked at her again. "You're doing what you need to do to stay safe. Jacob needs you alive and well. You need to be strong for him now, and that means making smart decisions. When the storm passes, we'll get you down the mountain. Until then, you need to prepare and take care of yourself."

Fox nodded, though the tightness in his chest remained. "I know you're right. It's just... so hard to sit here and do nothing."

"You're not doing nothing." Max pointed at the tool bag in front of him. "You're preparing. You're getting ready so you can be there for Jacob when the time comes. That's not nothing, Fox. That's love. And it's what Jacob needs from you right now."

Fox took a deep breath, trying to steady himself. "I just hope he can hold on until I get there."

"He will." Max gave him a shaky smile. "Jacob's a fighter. He'll hold on. And you'll be there for him when he wakes up."

Fox felt a flicker of hope at Max's words. He knew she was right—Jacob was strong, and he needed to be strong for him too. He had to trust that his brother would fight through this, and he had to be ready to support him when he did.

Max helped him gather the rest of his supplies, her eyes flicking to him every time he stopped and looked towards the window. She knew he wanted nothing more than to rush headlong into the storm to get to his brother and she hoped, for his sake, that the storm would pass by quickly. They worked in silence for a while, the only sounds were the crackling of the fire and the wind picking up strength outside. Once everything was packed and ready, Fox sat down by the fire, his mind still racing but his heart a little lighter.

Max eased down to sit next to him, her hand

resting on his arm. "He'll be okay, Fox. You have to believe that."

He looked at her and swallowed hard before speaking. "What if I'm the reason he wrecked?"

Max cocked her head to the side and looked at him with uncertainty. "What do you mean?"

Returning his attention to the fire, he spoke softly as if talking to himself. "Kendall said he wrecked six days ago. That's the last time he sent me a text. When I responded, he never replied. What if that's what caused the wreck?"

Max was shaking her head even though he wasn't looking at her. "You can't think like that, Fox. You said yourself, they don't know what caused the wreck."

His eyes were damp when he looked over at her. "But what if..."

"Fox? The *what ifs* will drive you crazy until you can get an answer from Jacob. Try to focus on what you know instead and on him getting better." After a brief hesitation, Fox nodded, and she scooted closer until she could wrap her arm around his waist and lay her head on his shoulder.

They sat in silence for a while, the warmth of the fire a comforting presence. Fox's thoughts drifted to Jacob again, but this time he felt a little more hopeful. He pictured his brother's face, imagined him waking up, and vowed to be there for him, no matter what it took.

As night fell, the storm intensified, the wind battering the cabin and snow piling up against the windows. Fox dozed fitfully, jerking awake at every creak and groan of the old wood. He kept his gear ready, his mind on high alert despite his exhaustion. Every minute felt like an eternity, the waiting making him anxious as the night slowly crept towards morning.

twelve

The cabin creaked softly with the weight of the storm outside, its walls barely containing the swirl of emotions within. Fox stood by the window, his gaze fixed on the relentless cascade of snowflakes. Max sat by the fire, her hands clutching a warm mug of coffee, her eyes distant yet searching.

Fox finally broke the silence, his voice rough with unspoken turmoil. "Max. I have to find a way off this mountain."

She turned to look at him, her heart sinking even as she nodded slowly. The fire cast flickering shadows across her face, accentuating the lines of worry etched there. "I know."

His jaw tightened, the weight of the decision pressing down on him. "Your car is the only way down." His voice was strained as he spoke. "But it's not equipped for this. If I wait, the snow might clear enough to drive, but..."

"But Jacob needs you now," Max finished for him, her voice trembling slightly.

Fox closed his eyes briefly, fighting the swell of emotions threatening to engulf him. "I can't wait too long. Every moment matters."

Silence settled between them once more, heavy and charged with unspoken fears. Max traced the rim of her mug with a finger, her thoughts racing with conflicting desires. She had come to care deeply for Fox, his strength and compassion weaving their way into her heart. But now, faced with the prospect of losing him to the storm, she struggled to reconcile her own longing with the urgency of him needing to be by Jacob's side.

"I want you to go." Dropping her gaze to her lap, she swallowed down her fear and spoke softly. "Jacob needs you. I understand."

Fox stepped closer, his hand reaching out to gently lift her chin, forcing her to meet his gaze. "Max, I..."

"Don't." Shaking her head, she reached up and laid her hand over his wrist, giving it a slight squeeze as she spoke. "Don't apologize for wanting to be there for your brother. I couldn't ask you to stay. No. Let me rephrase that. I would never ask you to stay if you can get to him safely."

He held her gaze for a long moment, gratitude and regret mingling in his eyes. "Thank you, for understanding." Leaning forward, he placed a gentle kiss on her trembling lips before straightening and looking back towards the window.

Tears welled in her eyes, her heart heavy with the weight of the decision he made. She squeezed his hand tightly, silently fighting the need to beg him to stay.

As if sensing her unspoken words, he looked down at her and tightened his grip on her hand, gently tugging her hand until she was standing next to him. "I'll be back as soon as I can." His voice was firm as he made a promise he didn't know if he'd be able to keep.

Max nodded, a tear slipping down her cheek. "I just need you to be safe, Fox."

They stood together, hands still intertwined, their gazes locked as they listened to the storm raging outside. The wind howled relentlessly, and ice tapped against the windowpanes.

Stepping forward, Max wrapped her arms around Fox's waist and laid her head against his chest, her eyes closing slowly as she listened to the beating of his heart. "Promise me you'll wait until full daylight to leave."

Fox gave her a slight squeeze and kissed the top of her head. "I can't make you that promise, Max. As soon as the storm passes, I have to head out. I have to make it down the mountain before it starts up again."

She stiffened in his arms briefly before nodding and hugging him tighter. "Wake me before you go?" When she felt him nod, she released him and stepped back, smiling softly before limping down the hall to her room.

As night deepened into morning, Fox prepared for his departure, pulling the sweatpants Max had given him on over his jeans and checking his gear with meticulous care. Max watched him silently, her heart aching with both fear and a fierce, unspoken hope. She knew this was the right choice, the only choice, yet the weight of their separation hung heavy in the air. "Wait." Hurrying as fast as her leg would allow, she went into her room and came back a few minutes later with two pairs of thick wool socks. "Take these."

Fox looked down at the socks, his mouth twitching

up at the corner. "Thanks, but I don't think they will fit me."

Tapping his chest with them, she smirked before dropping them into his tool bag. "They are for your hands, bud."

Catching her by the waist, Fox pulled her close and cupped her cheek before dropping a kiss onto the tip of her nose. "You keep the fire going while I'm gone. I don't won't anything else happening to you."

Max nodded but remained silent, savoring the feel of his arms wrapped around her.

When dawn broke, the storm showed no signs of relenting, but Fox was ready. He stood by the door, his backpack slung over his shoulder, his gaze fixed on Max with a mixture of longing and determination.

"I'll come back for you." His voice was steady despite the mixed emotions swirling within him.

Max nodded, her voice barely a whisper. "I'll be here."

With a final, lingering glance, Fox stepped into the swirling snow, disappearing into the blinding whiteness that enveloped the mountain. Max watched him until he vanished from sight, her heart torn between the ache of his absence and the quiet pride of knowing he was doing what he must.

Alone in the cabin, she moved to the window, her

breath misting the glass as she watched snowflakes dance in the wind. Her thoughts drifted to Fox, to Jacob, and to the possibility that she may never see either of them again. When tears filled her eyes again, she let them fall unchecked, her hand rubbing absently between her breasts as a pinching pain filled her chest.

thirteen

The wind whipped around Fox relentlessly as he trudged through the thick blanket of snow. Every step was a battle against the biting cold that seeped through his clothes, chilling him to the bone. His fingers, despite being gloved, felt stiff and numb, the skin on his face stung from the biting wind. Yet, he pressed on, driven by the desperate need to reach Jacob.

Night fell with a cruel descent, plunging the world into an icy darkness. Fox struggled to find shelter, his breath coming out in ragged puffs as he scanned the landscape for any sign of safety. The cold gnawed at him, threatening frostbite with each passing minute. He stumbled upon a shallow cave, barely large enough to shield him from the snow and brutal wind.

Huddling in the cramped space, he used every ounce of willpower to keep warm through the long, bitter night.

Morning brought a slight reprieve as the sun peeked timidly over the horizon. Fox, stiff and sore, emerged from his makeshift shelter. He knew he had to keep moving despite the ache in his muscles and the burning cold that still clung to him. With renewed determination, he pushed forward, his mind solely focused on reaching Jacob.

Hours passed like an eternity as Fox navigated treacherous terrain, his body weary but his spirit relentless. Finally, he saw the faint glimmer of lights, indicating he was nearing the foot of the mountain. With a surge of hope, he quickened his pace, each step bringing him closer to the highway.

When he reached the road, he turned towards the town and picked up his pace, hoping someone would drive by and offer him a ride.

By the time Fox reached the hospital, exhaustion weighed heavily on him, mingling with relief and worry for Jacob. He pushed open the doors, the warmth of the hospital a welcome relief from the frigid mountain air. A nurse noticed him immediately, her brow furrowing with concern as she took in his wind-burned face and shaking hands.

"Fox, are you alright?" Her voice was gentle, tinged with worry as she ushered him towards a chair. "Don't tell me you came down from the mountain in this weather."

Fox managed a weak smile, the adrenaline wearing off now that he was safe. "I need to see Jacob. He was brought in a about a week ago."

The nurse nodded, her expression softening with sympathy. "Let me check for you. Please, have a seat. You must be freezing."

Fox sank into the chair, the tension in his shoulders easing slightly as he waited. His mind raced with thoughts of Jacob, and he silently prayed that he wasn't too late.

After what felt like an eternity, the nurse returned with a reassuring smile. "Jacob is stable. He's still unconscious, but the doctors are hopeful."

Relief flooded through Fox, overwhelming him for a moment. "Can I see him?"

"Of course. Follow me."

She led Fox down a maze of corridors, the sterile hospital smells and the quiet hum of machinery a stark contrast to the wild solitude of the mountain. They stopped outside a room where Jacob lay, pale and still, hooked up to various monitors. Fox approached the bed with cautious steps, his heart heavy with worry and guilt.

When he spoke, Fox's voice was hoarse with emotion. "I'm here, Jake." He reached out, gripping Jacob's hand gently. "I'm sorry I couldn't get to you sooner."

Silence filled the room, broken only by the steady beep of the heart monitor. Pulling over a chair, Fox sat by Jacob's side, silently urging his brother to fight for his life.

For ten long days, he took turns with Kendall watching over Jacob. As much as he wanted to return to Mirror Springs Mountain and Max, he knew his place was here, beside his brother.

When Jacob finally regained consciousness, and they knew he'd make a full recovery, Kendall insisted that Fox return to the mountain to check on Max.

Reassuring his brother that he'd be back by the

weekend, Fox left the hospital and made his way to the diner. Stepping inside, he nodded at Darlene and waited for her to reach his side before he spoke. "You think Troy will lend me his snowcat for a few days?"

"I don't see why not. How's Jacob, by the way?" Picking up the coffee carafe, she poured some of the hot liquid into a to-go cup and passed it across the counter to Fox.

"On the road to recovery. Barring any complications, he should be going home in the next week or two." Taking a sip of the coffee, he sighed and glanced around the empty diner. "Not busy today?"

"We get a few stragglers every now and again." Pointing towards a door behind the counter, she began wiping down the menus as she spoke. "Troy's upstairs with the baby. You can go on up and ask him about the snowcat."

Pulling two twenties from his pocket, he tossed them on the counter on his way to the door.

"Fox, you..."

"I'd like two triple burger specials to go and use whatever is left to pay for the next customer. Thanks for the joe, darlin'."

Shaking her head, she picked up the bills and dropped them in the pocket of her apron as she turned towards the kitchen.

fourteen

The blazing fire in the cabin's hearth cast dancing shadows across the room as Max sat on the couch, her mind a whirlwind of emotions. Outside, the snow continued to fall, but inside, a different storm brewed within her chest. She had barely managed to calm herself after Fox's return, his presence both a comfort and a reminder of the truth she had kept hidden from him for too long.

She heard Fox moving about the cabin, stoking the fire and shedding layers of winter gear. Her heart sank with each passing moment of silence between them, knowing she couldn't keep him in the dark any longer. The fear of losing him mingled with the fear of facing her own mortality, a weight she couldn't bear alone any longer.

When Fox finally settled beside her on the couch, concern etched deep lines on his face. His eyes searched hers, wordlessly urging her to open up, to tell him what was bothering her. "What's wrong? You've been quiet since I got here."

Max took a deep breath, steeling herself against his reaction to what she was about to tell him. "Fox..." His name came out as a squeak and she cleared her throat before speaking again, her voice trembling slightly despite her efforts to remain composed. "There's something I need to tell you."

He turned to face her fully, his expression a mixture of apprehension and concern. "What is it, Max?" His voice was gentle, yet there was an underlying urgency that spoke volumes.

Max swallowed hard, her fingers twisting nervously in her lap. "I... I have coronary artery disease." She forced herself to hold his gaze as she continued, each word heavy with the weight of her secret. "I'm sorry, I know I should have told you sooner."

Fox's eyes widened in shock, his breath catching in his throat. "Why are you telling me now? Are you okay? Do you need to go to the hospital?" His voice held a note of desperation, his hands reaching out to grasp hers in a tight, reassuring grip.

Tears welled up in Max's eyes as she met his gaze,

her heart breaking at the hurt she had caused him. "I'm fine. I had a few pains the day you left but they passed on their own."

"Why didn't you tell me sooner?"

Letting her gaze drop to their clasped hands, she spoke in a hoarse whisper. "I didn't want to burden you with my problems. And, later, when I got to know you better, I was scared... scared of losing you if you knew."

Fox's grip on her hands tightened, his voice filled with a mix of frustration and concern. "Max, you shouldn't have kept something like this from me." When she looked back up, his eyes searched hers with unwavering intensity. "You need to see a doctor, get proper care..."

Max nodded her head, tears slipping down her cheeks unchecked. "I know. I'm sorry I didn't tell you sooner, I just..."

When her words trailed off, Fox pulled her into his arms, holding her close against his chest. "I'm here now," he murmured against her hair, his voice a soothing balm to her frayed nerves. "And I'm not going anywhere."

Max clung to him, feeling the weight of her fear and guilt lift slightly in the warmth of his embrace. "Are you mad at me?" Her voice muffled against his shoulder, and she raised her head and asked again. "Are you mad?"

Shaking his head, he held her tighter, his hands gentle yet firm. "I'm not mad. But promise me you'll see a doctor as soon as you can."

Max nodded against his chest, a sense of relief washing over her as she leaned into his strength. In that moment, standing together in the middle of the cabin they had worked so hard to repair and feeling the warmth of Fox's arms around her, she knew in the time they had been trapped in the cabin, that she had fallen for the handyman. A smile touched her lips, and she leaned back to look up at him. Her gaze roved over his face until she finally looked into his eyes and spoke the words she had been waiting to tell him. "I love you, Fox. You don't have to respond. I just needed to tell you that." Closing her eyes, she rested her head back on his chest, but had she been looking at him still, she would've seen the smile of wonder that crept across his face.

fifteen

The warmth of summer had transformed the once snow-covered landscape into a lush green paradise around Max's cabin. Sunlight filtered through the leaves, casting playful patterns on the porch where Max stood, a radiant smile gracing her face. Inside, the cabin was filled with soft music and the scent of the cake she had baked earlier. Max waved as Jacob and Kendall, accompanied by Fox, arrived for a long-awaited visit.

Jacob, ever the charismatic troublemaker, sauntered into the cabin with Kendall on his arm, a mischievous twinkle in his eye that hadn't dimmed despite the woman standing at his side. "Max, you've really turned this place into a gem." His gaze swept appreciatively over the improvements Max and Fox had made.

Max beamed with pride, gesturing around the cozy interior. "Thanks, Jacob. It's been a labor of love."

Kendall nodded in agreement, her smile warm and genuine. "It's absolutely beautiful, Max. You and Fox have done an amazing job."

Fox stood beside Max, his hand lightly resting on her lower back, a silent testament to their growing bond. Max couldn't help but steal glances at him, her heart skipping a beat each time their eyes met. She longed for the evening ahead, knowing Fox had something special planned.

As they toured the cabin, Max couldn't resist the urge to touch Fox—a hand on his arm here, fingers brushing his cheek there—unable to contain the joy and affection that bubbled within her. Fox reciprocated with gentle touches and loving glances, their unspoken connection speaking volumes of their deepening love.

Later that evening, at their favorite lakeside restaurant, the atmosphere was charged with anticipation. The sun dipped low on the horizon, casting a golden glow over the water as they enjoyed a leisurely meal together.

Fox stole covert glances at Max throughout the evening, his heart pounding with nerves and excitement. He had planned every detail meticulously, from the secluded table with a view of the lake to the heartfelt words he would speak.

As dessert arrived, Fox's hand found Max's across the table, their fingers intertwining as he gazed deeply into her eyes. "Max," he began, his voice soft yet filled with determination. "These past months with you have been the happiest of my life. You've brought so much light and love into my world, and I can't imagine a future without you."

Max's breath caught in her throat, tears of happiness welling in her eyes as she listened to Fox pour out his heart. This was the moment she had hoped for, the moment she would catch herself daydreaming about as she worked in her new garden or while cooking him dinner.

He smiled at her nervously as he slid a small velvet box across the table, revealing a shimmering diamond ring that sparkled in the fading sunlight. "Will you marry me, Max?"

Overwhelmed with emotion, Max nodded fervently, unable to find her voice as Fox slipped the ring onto her finger. Cheers erupted from nearby tables as they shared a tender kiss, their hearts overflowing with love and joy.

As they walked hand in hand along the lake shore after dinner, the last rays of sunlight painting the sky in hues of pink and gold, Max leaned into Fox's embrace, knowing that their love had weathered winter storms and blossomed in the warmth of summer. The cabin in the woods, once a place of fear and isolation, had become a place of joy and happiness where their dreams would flourish, side by side, for the rest of their lives.

**I'd love to know what you thought of
Mended Hearts**

Thank you for purchasing **Mended Hearts**.
I am extremely grateful to everyone that made
the decision to purchase and read one of my
books.
I hope that it was everything you hoped it
would be. It would be really nice if you could
share this book with your friends and family by
posting to **Facebook, Instagram** or by
creating a **TikTok** video.
If you enjoyed this book I'd like to hear from
you and hope that you could take some time to
post a review on **Amazon** and/or **Goodreads.**

about the author

Greer Rylie is from small town Arkansas and has been happily married for 24 years, showing her commitment to her Southern values. She loves cooking and makes delicious Southern dishes in her kitchen. She also enjoys taking photos, capturing beautiful moments. Greer cares deeply about animals, which reflects her kind personality. She's written four books, and has several more planned to be released at a later date. She dreams of becoming a best-selling author and sharing her stories with more people. Join Greer on her journey as she continues to write the stories she hopes you'll fall in love with.

facebook.com/GreerRylie.Author

tiktok.com/@greer.rylieauthor21

amazon.com/Greer-Rylie/e/B09NCKP6C3

instagram.com/greer_rylie_writes